I panicked. I nearly dropped Meatball's leash and ran away up the street. Instead I said, "Let's go, Meatball!" and started walking as fast as I could.

My arm was practically yanked out of its socket as I reached the end of the leash.

Meatball had planted himself on the sidewalk in front of Rebekah's house. I mean, it was like he'd grown roots right there. His paws were braced against the concrete. His shoulders were hunched. His face was stubborn. He was leaning his whole weight back against the end of the leash, and he wasn't going anywhere.

I was in big trouble.

Get into some

Pet Trouble

Runaway Retriever

Loudest Beagle on the Block

Mud-Puddle Poodle

Bulldog Won't Budge

Oh No, Newf!

Pet Trouble

Bulldog Won't Budge

by T. T. SUTHERLAND

SCHOLASTIC INC.
New York Toronto London Auckland Sydney
Mexico City New Delhi Hong Kong Buenos Aires

ISBN-13: 978-0-545-10300-8
ISBN-10: 0-545-10300-2

12 11 10 9 8 7 6 5 4 3 2 1 9 10 11 12 13 14/0

Printed in the U.S.A.
First printing, November 2009

For Rebekah and Ellie

CHAPTER 1

Dr. Lee," said my friend Parker, "how come you guys don't have a dog?"

"*Good question*," I said. "Yeah, Mom, how come we don't have a dog?"

The funny thing is, Parker was being kind of psychic right then, but no one knew it yet. I mean, not psychic in that weird fake way that Cadence Bly is — she's in the sixth grade with us, and she's always pretending to "sense the vibrations of the universe" or something. But Parker really was practically seeing the future, like he could sense what was sitting outside waiting for us. Like magic.

But he didn't know that, and I didn't know that, and neither did Mom. It seemed like just an ordinary rainy Monday. We were at my mom's office — she's one of the vets at the Paws and Claws Animal Hospital in our town. I like visiting her there because it's really clean and sometimes she lets me hang out with the dogs that are staying overnight for surgery. Plus my big sisters never come to the office unless they're bringing in their cats. Mercy and Faith are sixteen and they're kind of mean when they're mad (which is most of the time), so I try to stay out of their way. They like me about as much as they like boiled turnips or going back to school after Christmas.

The animal hospital has smooth white tile floors and framed posters of dogs and cats all over the sky blue and sunshine yellow walls. Most of the posters have quotes on them like "My goal in life is to be as good a person as my dog thinks I am" and "Dogs have owners, cats have staff." My favorite is this photograph of a black Lab with his front paws on a computer keyboard, looking at the camera like *Do you have an appointment? I'm very busy here.*

It was near the end of the day, so we were the only ones still there. Even Cassie, the receptionist with the pierced nose, had gone home. She's nice, but she always seems really bored, which I don't understand, because she gets to see dogs all day long, and I think that would never get boring.

I was sitting at Mom's computer, messing with her screen saver. Parker and his dad had brought Parker's new dog, Merlin, in for a checkup. Mom was doing all the regular vet things like *tsk-tsk*ing at his teeth and sticking a thermometer up his butt. Poor Merlin!

That must be the worst thing about being a dog. OK, that and having to pee outside in January, when it's freezing.

Parker Green is one of my best friends, along with Danny Sanchez and Troy Morris. Parker got Merlin right before school started, and he's pretty much a perfect dog. (Mom says so, too, and she's kind of an expert.) Parker jokes about what a pain he can be, but the truth is he thinks Merlin is, like, King Arthur come back to life as a golden retriever. He's spent nearly every minute with his dog from the moment he got him, which was OK by me and Danny and Troy, because we all wanted dogs, too. Especially if we all could get dogs like Merlin.

"But Eric, we have Odysseus and Ariadne," Mom pointed out, like she always does.

And like I always do, I said, "Mom, cats are not the same as dogs. Especially when they are evil cats. That's like saying, 'Honey, you don't need a Wii, because we've got this lovely school of piranhas instead.'"

Parker laughed. He's been over to my house enough, so he knows what my sisters' cats are like. He once made the mistake of eating a tuna fish sandwich in our kitchen, and the cats have never forgiven him. Whenever he comes over, they follow him around the house glaring at him. Ariadne and Odysseus believe pretty strongly that tuna is for cats only.

"Cats aren't evil," Mom said, shining a little light into Merlin's ears. Merlin was sitting up on this tall metal table and he looked really confused about it. He kept peering over the edge like he was thinking about jumping down. Parker was on the other side of the table from Mom, holding on to Merlin's collar to make sure he didn't run away. That's the only semi-bad thing Merlin ever does — he's a master escape artist, just like Houdini. But usually Merlin's running *to* Parker, not away from him, so I wasn't very worried.

"I know *most* cats aren't evil," I said. "Just ours."

I'm serious. I've met lots of good cats, especially when I'm hanging out in my mom's office and they come in for checkups. My cousins have a really cute kitten named Gergen, who likes to play and get petted, and he's as funny as any dog. There's a guy on our baseball team, Levi Axelrod, who has a fat white Persian cat that is totally chill and purrs like a locomotive the minute you touch her. Plus Rebekah Waters in our class absolutely loves cats. Any cat that belonged to her couldn't possibly be evil. If we had a cat like that — purring and friendly and not-evil — maybe it wouldn't be so bad.

But Odysseus and Ariadne hate everyone, except maybe Mercy and Faith. They like to sit up on high things and glare at me. (The cats, I mean. Well, OK, my sisters, too.) If I get too close to the cats, they scratch me. I have to keep my bedroom door shut all the time because whenever they can get into my room, they pee on my bed. Yeah, it's mega gross.

I have no idea what I did to make them hate me so much. It's not like I ever pulled their tails or shut them in the shower, like some guys I know would have (like, say, Avery Lafitte, biggest jerk in the sixth grade). I'm totally harmless. Maybe they think I'm some kind of secret tuna fish thief. Or maybe they can just smell how much I want a dog.

"You know, Danny has a dog now, too," Parker said to his dad. He kind of looks like his dad, although mostly it's in the way they wrinkle their foreheads when they're worried or shrug their shoulders when they're trying to get out of an argument.

"Really?" Mr. Green said. "Since when?"

"I don't know," Parker said, scratching behind Merlin's ears. "We just found out a couple days ago. We ran into his sister at the park."

"He was embarrassed to tell us because it's a toy poodle," I said. "But she's really cute. Mom, I don't even care if it's a little dog. Any kind of dog would be OK."

"Scoot," she said, grabbing the back of her chair as I was spinning around in it. "I need to type up Merlin's receipt and prescription."

Mom is an expert at dodging subjects she wants to avoid. Like this conversation, which we'd been having for maybe a year, but more often in the month since Parker got Merlin.

As she sat down, she raised her eyebrows at her new screen saver. A quotation was scrolling across the screen: "No performer should attempt to bite off red-hot iron unless he has a good set of teeth. — Harry Houdini."

"Er — what good advice," Mom said.

"I found it online," I said. I like reading about Harry Houdini. He was the bravest person ever. I could never get up in front of an audience like he did — never mind the part where he jumped into lakes wrapped in chains!

"Yes, well, I'd like my slide-show screen saver back before you leave, please," Mom said, clicking through to her files. "I'm afraid this one might confuse my patients."

"OK," I said, "but all those scrolling photos of dogs confuse *me*, the person who can't have one."

"We'll get a dog one day," Mom said. "When we come across the right one." She checked her watch. "For now, Eric, will you go out front and flip the sign to 'Closed'? Make sure the emergency numbers are showing through the window."

"Sure." I patted Merlin's head as I went by and he licked my hand. I could hear Mom explaining heartworm pills to Parker and his dad as I went through the waiting room. There were a couple of animal magazines lying on the dark blue plastic seats, so I put them back on the side tables and straightened them while I was out there. I also noticed a couple of dog biscuits lying on the floor — someone must have dropped them when they got up with their dog. I put them in my jacket pocket to give to Merlin later. It may not surprise you to hear that dogs really, really don't care if their food has been dropped on the floor.

The animal hospital has an inner door and then a vestibule with an outer door, which it shares with the pet shop next door. The pet shop was already closed for the day. It was nearly dinnertime. I went out into the vestibule and saw through the glass walls that it was starting to get dark already, even though it was only the end of September. But I like it when that starts happening because it means winter is coming. I know, it's weird to like winter, but I do.

Snow is better than rain, anyhow. The rain was pattering down outside, leaving shiny wet trails along the glass like melting diamonds. I went to the outer door to flip over the CLOSED sign.

And that's when I saw the dog.

CHAPTER 2

I pressed my nose to the glass door, squinting through the rain.

There was a bulldog sitting right outside. He was staring in at me just like I was staring out at him.

I've never seen a glummer face. I mean, I think that's kind of a funny word — "glum" — but that was the first thought that popped into my head when I saw this dog's face. He wasn't just sad. He wasn't gloomy. He was definitely glum.

His little dark brown ears drooped. His big, broad shoulders drooped. His long, floppy jowls drooped. His forehead was wrinkled in a worried way, and his sad brown eyes seemed to be saying *Why am I so wet? And so alone? And so abandoned? And so very, very wet?*

For a moment I thought he was just hanging out on the sidewalk for no reason. But then I realized that he was wearing a red leash — and the leash was tied to the vestibule's front door.

I thought I should run back and get my mom. But I didn't want to leave him in the pouring rain even one second longer. I pulled open the inner door and yelled "MOM!" really loudly. Then I let it close and went to push open the outer door.

The bulldog sat up a little straighter, looking at me hopefully. The brown-and-white fur on his neck stood up in little wet spikes. I untangled his leash from the door handle, which was sort of tough because it was pretty wet and slippery. I had to stand in the rain and get totally drenched. But I got it free, and then I held the door open and beckoned to the dog.

"Come on boy," I said.

He didn't need any more encouragement than that. He rocketed inside so quickly, he nearly bowled me over. He stood inside our vestibule and shook and shook himself. His jowls went *flap-flap-flap-flap-flap.* He sprayed me all over with water, but it didn't matter because I was already wet. My sneakers went *squeak-squish-squeak-squish* as I tried to wring out my shirt without taking it off.

The bulldog's wheezing and snorting echoed around the vestibule. He looked up at me with big trusting eyes — that's the kind of look my mom gets from the sweetest dogs when they're like *Maybe if I look really pathetic you'll put away that needle.* Like he was afraid I would leave and he was hoping if he looked really woebegone I'd stay with him.

I realized that there was a piece of paper folded and tucked into his collar, under his chin. I crouched down to reach for it, and the dog came over and butted my hand with his head. I scratched behind his ears and under his broad chin until I could reach the note, and then I pulled it out. But when I stopped petting the dog, he plowed into my knees and I fell back on my butt. This was apparently exactly what he hoped would happen. He immediately tried to climb into my lap and lick my chin.

Danny's dog, Buttons, had done the same thing at the park on Sunday, but Buttons is a puppy the size of a baseball and she weighs about as much as one. This was a full-grown bulldog, and he was *heavy*. I swear he felt like he weighed as much as me. His big white paws planted themselves on my chest and his enormous pink tongue went *sluuuuuuuurrrrrp!* up the side of my face like a giant piece of wet sandpaper.

I tried to push him off, but he was really, really determined to show me how glad he was to be in out of the rain. He was like *I must pin you down and say thank you by licking off your face! How else will you know how grateful I am?!* I could feel his tiny stub of a tail wagging up the whole length of his wet, roly-poly body.

"OK!" I cried as he licked me again. "I get it! You're welcome!"

The inside door opened. "Eric?" my mom said as she came out. "Did you — oh my goodness!" Her mouth fell open. She stared at the bulldog, who was flopped across my chest. He looked up at her with a panting, slobbering grin. His tongue was as wide as my hand and it flapped up and down as he breathed, *FLAP HUFF FLAP HUFF FLAP HUFF.*

"Where — what —?" My mom pointed at the bulldog. "Eric!"

"He was sitting outside," I said. "In the rain, Mom! Someone left him tied to the front door."

"Tied to the front door?" Mom sounded indignant now.

"In the *rain*," I said again.

I saw Parker and Mr. Green crowd up behind her. Merlin poked his nose through the gap between their legs. His eyes lit up when he saw the bulldog, but Parker held on to him so he couldn't rush forward and say hi.

"There's a note," I said, holding it out so Mom could rescue it from me. I needed my other hand to fend off the slobbermeister.

"Check his tags," she said as she unfolded it. I wrestled the dog's giant head aside so I could see the plain black collar hidden in the folds of his neck. There was only one tag hanging from it, a silver one shaped like a dog bone. And all it said was "Meatball."

"Meatball?" I said to him. He buried his whole wet face in my neck and went *snorftle snorftle*, so I guess that was a yes.

"'Please take care of Meatball,'" my mom read out loud. The paper was soggy and falling apart in her hands. "'We cannot have him anymore. Thank you.'" She threw her hands up. "Of course it isn't signed! They're lucky I can't find them and tell them what I think of them. This poor dog. I'm sure they just thought he was an adorable puppy and had no idea how big he would get."

"Or how loud," I said as Meatball went *SNOOOOOORRRRRG* right in my ear.

"Why would they bring him here instead of an animal shelter?" Mr. Green asked. "Do you know him?"

Mom shook her head. "I've never seen him before. I haven't had any bulldogs in here this year. I wouldn't be surprised if they drove over from another town. One of my colleagues online told me about a dog left at her office, too — like they figure a vet must know how to take care of it."

"And they guess a vet would want to," Parker pointed out.

I'd finally managed to sit up, but Meatball had planted himself firmly in my lap and was snuffling up and down my chest with his big squashed-up nose. His forehead was wrinkled forward over his serious brown eyes. He shoved his head inside my jacket. I scratched the folds of wrinkles around his neck. His fur wasn't long and smooth like Merlin's. It felt soft and prickly at the same time, like running your hand over newly mown grass. Well — really *wet* newly mown grass. Meatball was absolutely soaked. I wondered how long he'd been sitting outside.

"Let's bring him inside and scan him for a microchip," Mom said.

"A microchip?" Parker said with a grin. "You mean, he might be a robot dog?"

"Yeah, right," I said. "No one would make a robot dog this slobbery."

Mom grabbed Meatball's collar and wrestled him off me. He leaned against her leg as I stood up, but when she relaxed her grip on his collar, he lunged away from her and barreled into my knees again. I managed to stay upright, but he seemed really determined to climb back inside my jacket.

"You should get Merlin microchipped, too," Mom said to Mr. Green. "Then if he ever gets lost, the vet or shelter who finds him will be able to trace him back to you. It's a simple injection, and a good precaution."

"Especially with a runaway maniac like you," Parker said, ruffling Merlin's fur. Merlin gave him an adoring look and wagged his long golden tail.

Mom tried tugging on Meatball's collar again, but he refused to move until I did. He stuck to my side as we went back into the waiting room. In my mom's office, he stopped and let Merlin sniff him up and down. Merlin's tail was going nuts, as if he'd just met his new best friend. Meanwhile, Meatball kept looking at me with his tongue hanging out in a goofy grin, like *Who does this guy think he is? And what's he so excited about?*

It took me and Parker together to heave Meatball off the floor and onto the examination table. The dog didn't help either; he wriggled and flailed and tried to climb inside my jacket again and it was totally just like wrestling a wet walrus.

Finally we got him onto the metal table and he immediately lay down and flopped over with his head as close to me as he could get it. His breathing was really loud, like snorting and wheezing and gasping and growling all at once. I rubbed his solid white belly while Mom looked for a microchip.

"Of course not," she muttered. "Does nobody want you, poor boy?" She tugged on one of his floppy ears. Meatball rolled onto his stomach, wiggled toward me, and pawed at my jacket, which by this point was covered in little wet brown-and-white dog hairs.

"Oh, I'm an idiot," I said, realizing why he loved my jacket so much. I pulled out one of the dog biscuits I'd found in the waiting room. "Is this what you're looking for?" I said, offering it to him.

"Careful," Mom said, taking it from me. "Bulldogs often have really narrow throats. You have to make sure to break up their treats into small, bite-sized pieces." She snapped the biscuit into a few little chunks and handed it back to me. Meatball kept his big brown eyes fixed raptly on the biscuit as it went back and forth between us. His jowls wobbled as he swung his head from one side to the other. But he waited patiently until I held out my hand with the treat in it.

SNORF. The biscuit disappeared in a whoosh of crunching and slurping. Meatball licked the palm of my hand a few times for good measure, leaving it damp and sticky. His stumpy tail was wriggling with the rest of him.

"I'll call Wags to Whiskers and see if they have room for him tonight," Mom said, sliding her chair over to the office phone. Meatball rested his big head on the table and turned his enormous eyes up to me with this massively woeful expression.

"Wait," I said. "Can't we take him home with us? Please, Mom? Look how much he likes us."

Meatball helpfully rolled over and gave her a winning upside-down grin. All the wrinkles in his face got deeper as his eyes crinkled up, just like a person smiling. His big pink tongue had a crease down the middle as if it had been folded in half to fit inside his mouth.

Mom put her hands on her hips and sighed. "We don't know anything about him, Eric. We don't know if he has fleas, or if he's aggressive to cats, or if he's sick —"

"So check him," I suggested. "You can figure out most of that stuff, right? Poor Meatball. He's had such a bad day. His people left him all alone in the rain. You don't want him to sleep on the floor in a lonely cage tonight, do you?"

Mom gave Mr. Green one of those grown-up looks. Parker's dad shrugged. "I'd have trouble saying no to either of those faces," he said, nodding at me and Meatball. Parker is like his dad that way, too; he never says no to anything either.

"It's just for the night," Parker added helpfully. "Then you can figure out what to do with him in the morning. One night can't hurt, right?" He looked innocent, but I knew he was thinking what I was thinking — if we could just get one night now, maybe we could get more later.

Mom was totally onto us, but she knew she was beaten. "One night," she said with a sigh. "And I'll check him over first. Eric, call your sisters and tell them we'll be late for dinner."

Parker followed me out to the waiting room and high-fived me. "Maybe this is it," he said. "Maybe you finally have a dog!" Merlin barked in agreement and Parker scratched his ears.

"Yeah," I said, thinking about how fat and funny-looking Meatball was next to sleek, perfect Merlin.

"E-mail me later and let me know what happens," Parker said. He clipped Merlin's leash on and waved as they followed his dad out the front door.

I looked at the phone for a minute after they left, wondering if I'd done the right thing. I hadn't really thought about *keeping* Meatball, like, *forever* and ever. He wasn't exactly the dog I'd always pictured for myself. When I thought about dogs, I pictured Labs and collies and Weimaraners and Great Danes — big, long-legged, athletic dogs. I didn't know anyone with a bulldog. I'd never thought about having a dog with a squashed-up face and stubby legs and droopy jowls.

But I couldn't send him off to a shelter all by himself. Poor guy. I just wanted to give him somewhere warm and friendly to go. Did that mean we had to keep him? Was I stuck with him now?

I wondered why his owners had abandoned him. Was there something wrong with him? Or was *any* dog too much work for them?

I thought about his glum face through the raindrops. I don't know, maybe I was being stupid.

But even if Meatball wasn't the perfect dog for me, I knew *I* couldn't abandon him, too. No one should be left behind twice in one night.

CHAPTER 3

My sister Mercy was standing in the kitchen, behind the screen door, glowering at us as we came up the driveway. Her eyes went straight to Meatball, who was trotting cheerily beside me, on his leash. I'd mentioned on the phone that we were bringing home a dog, but then I'd hung up before she could yell at me.

My sisters are not exactly dog fans. They're cat people. In fact, they like cats a lot *more* than they like people (especially little brothers).

I could see Ariadne up on the counter behind Mercy, wearing the exact same displeased expression on her striped gray face. The cats aren't really allowed on the kitchen counters, but Mercy and Faith never stop them from going wherever they want, and I wouldn't dare try. I prefer my hands in their unshredded state.

"What is *that?"* Mercy asked through the screen door. I reached for the handle and she latched it shut from the inside.

"It's a bulldog," I said. "Come on, Mercy, let us in." Mom was still back at the car, digging out her piles of papers.

"You can't bring that thing in here," Mercy said, tossing her shiny, straight black hair. "It'll scare Ariadne."

Ariadne had been scaring *me* for eleven years, and I didn't see anyone doing anything about that.

"I'll make sure he leaves Ariadne alone," I said. Behind Mercy, the long-haired silver cat opened her jaws and hissed at me. I didn't think she'd even noticed Meatball yet. Although surely she could hear him. He was sitting patiently on my foot, panting like he'd just run a marathon. My sister wrinkled her nose as a bit of slobber dripped off his tongue.

"Faith!" she yelled.

My other sister, Mercy's identical twin, popped out of the pantry with a box of Wheat Thins in her hand. Her eyes narrowed when she saw Meatball. She came to stand next to Mercy and folded her arms. Now they were both blocking the door. They were both wearing jeans and white turtlenecks; Mercy's V-necked sweater was dark red and Faith's was tan with brown flecks.

They never wear exactly matching outfits, but they usually dress kind of alike, because they love confusing people and then pretending like they're really mad when someone gets them mixed up. I've told my friends the secret clue, for their own protection: Faith has a mole next to her nose, just below her left eye. That's how you can tell them apart, if you look carefully. Also, Mercy is just a little bit meaner and bossier than Faith, and Faith eats more, but those are probably easier to notice if you live with them.

"Look at that disgusting thing," said Mercy, wrinkling her nose at Meatball.

"It's horrible," Faith agreed.

"And the cats won't like it," Mercy pointed out.

"Odysseus has such delicate nerves," Faith observed.

Yeah, right, I thought.

"If we let it in, think of all the cleaning we'll have to do after we get rid of it tomorrow," Mercy said.

"*I* think it should sleep in the garage," said Faith.

"Me too," said Mercy. "Sorry Eric." (She wasn't sorry.) "It's two against one."

Yeah. It's always two against one in my house. Welcome to my whole entire life. Mercy and Faith were five when I was born, so they had a whole "gang up on him" plan in place, like, before I could even crawl. Our dad once admitted to me that they gave the girls kittens to "make up for" the fact that they had to put up with a little brother.

"He'll stay in my room," I said, although I felt like I was letting them win, as usual. "He won't bother the cats. Or you."

Faith snorted. This, by the way, was the longest conversation I'd had with either of them in months. We mostly avoid each other as much as possible.

"Eric?" My mom's voice came floating up the driveway. "What are you doing? Go in and give him some water." She'd given me a big speech on the way home about how easily bulldogs overheat, so you have to make sure to always have water around for them. And then she told me about cleaning his face wrinkles every day, which you have to do so they don't get infected. It all made me kind of nervous. I think she wanted me to be really, really sure I could take care of Meatball before I started pestering her to keep him. And maybe she wanted me to have second thoughts. Well, I was sure having them, whether she wanted me to or not.

I gave Mercy and Faith a shrug. "See? Mom says to let us in."

Faith stomped back into the pantry. Mercy rolled her eyes and flipped the latch on the screen door. She scooped Ariadne up in her arms and perched on one of the tall kitchen stools as I dropped Meatball's leash and held the screen door open for him.

He heaved himself over the doorstep and trotted cheerfully into the kitchen with his funny rolling walk. His front legs looked like wrinkled pants, with fat poofs of white paws at the ends. His shoulders were wider than his hips, and everything looked like it was rolling in a different direction when he walked.

I pulled out a Tupperware container and filled it with water for him, but he wasn't interested. He put his squashy black nose to the ground and snuffled across the tiles in a loud snorty way, peering over the top of his flat snout.

Mercy lifted her feet up to the highest rung and raised one eyebrow at Meatball as he snortled around her stool. She was holding Ariadne in what I call her "Dr. Evil" way. That's when the cat is stretched out along one arm while Mercy strokes her head with the other hand and they both look as sinister as possible.

Ariadne's back arched when she saw Meatball roll into view below her.

"HSSSSSSSSSSSSSS!" she spat.

Startled, Meatball spun around. He blinked right and then left. His small floppy ears were twitched forward. He stared around the kitchen and then gave me a confused look. His tongue flopped out and slurped across his nose.

I pointed at my sister and the cat. Meatball had to back up to see the top of the stool. But when he finally spotted Ariadne, his mouth dropped open and his tongue unfurled like a long pink carpet. His whole butt vibrated with excitement.

Needless to say, Ariadne was not quite so pleased to see *him*.

"Ew, gross! He's drooling on the floor!" Mercy said.

"Sorry," I said. I grabbed a paper towel and followed behind Meatball, wiping up the droplets, although he wasn't really *drooling*. I've seen drooling dogs (and cats!) at Mom's office and this wasn't too bad.

Mom banged through the door, carrying her briefcase and a bag of dog food she'd picked up at the office. They sell it in the animal hospital because that brand is really good for dogs' teeth. I took it from her and poured some into another Tupperware container for Meatball. *That* he was interested in. He stuck his whole face into the bowl and went *SNORF SNORF SNORFTYSNORFT SNORFTLE*, spraying crumbs and stray pellets everywhere as he ate. It was like he had to inhale the food and lap it up at the same time to get it inside his mouth, so there was no way to do it quietly . . . or neatly.

"Mom!" Mercy protested. "That is *so gross.*"

"Yeah," Faith chimed in, coming back out of the pantry. Now she was eating out of a bag of almonds. And if you ask me, she wasn't being any neater or quieter about it than poor Meatball. There were crumbs all over her sweater.

"It's not his fault," I said. "It's probably hard to eat with a face like that."

"It's probably hard to *live* with a face like that," Faith sniped, and Mercy snickered.

"Now, now," Mom said in her distracted way, checking her BlackBerry. "Where's Tony?"

Tony is my stepdad. He married my mom two years ago, although they'd dated almost since my parents' divorce six years ago, so we were pretty used to him by the time he moved in. He's a nice guy, although I think he's still working out how to be dadlike and how much he can boss us around. In our family, he's the "one of these things is not like the others." His parents came here from the Dominican Republic, and they still don't speak much English. Thanksgiving with them and Grandpa, who only speaks Chinese, is kind of hilarious.

"He's at another campaign meeting," said Mercy, reaching into Faith's bag of almonds. "He said they'd just have pizza there."

"That's the fourth time in a week," Mom said with an exasperated look. "That much pizza is not good for him."

"That much campaign talk isn't good for him, either," I added. Tony's on the city council and he wants to run for mayor next year. He's one of those people who everyone likes, so maybe he can actually beat Mayor Marvell, but right now we're all kind of like *OK, Tony, you go ahead.* None of the rest of us is exactly camera-friendly. I'm the last person you should put up on a stage to talk to people, unless what you're looking for is a lot of mumbling. And Mercy and Faith would probably claw a reporter's eyes out if they were asked any questions.

"Mom," Faith whined, "I'm hungry." She stuffed another fistful of almonds in her mouth.

"You girls could have started something for dinner," Mom said, looking flustered. She put down her BlackBerry and went to stare into the refrigerator. Meatball trotted up behind her and peered in at the stuffed shelves with rapturous attention.

"That dog better not slobber on our food," Mercy snapped.

"I'll take him upstairs," I said, grabbing his leash again.

That's when I first discovered Meatball's secret superpower. As I tried to lead him out of the kitchen, he braced his paws on the tiles, planted his butt on the floor, and *would not move.*

"Come on, Meatball," I said, tugging on his leash. He gave me an innocent look, then swiveled his massive head back toward the fridge. I tried pulling harder, but he didn't even seem to notice. Mercy and Faith were starting to laugh.

"Uh-oh," Mercy teased. "Eric's too scrawny for this dog."

"Figures," Faith added. "My arms are twice as big as his. Do you ever use those twigs for anything, Eric?"

"Let's have ravioli," Mom said, ignoring my sisters. She pulled a bag of frozen ravioli from the freezer and closed the fridge. Meatball looked disappointed. When I tugged on his leash he finally got up and lumbered along behind me into the hall and up the stairs.

I was a little worried that he'd have trouble with the stairs, since his body was so thick and his legs were so stubby, but he just kind of roll-galloped on up ahead of me, snorting excitedly. At the top his paws sank into the beige carpet and he put his nose down to the ground, burying it in the thick fibers.

Suddenly his head went up and his floppy ears twitched forward.

"Rrrrrrr . . . RRRFF!" he announced. It wasn't very loud; it was more like he was just letting me know about something.

I followed his gaze and realized that Faith's cat, Odysseus, was standing outside my room. He was crouched with one paw half raised like he'd frozen in mid-step. His yellow eyes were enormous in his feathery black face. His tail lashed back and forth as he stared at Meatball.

Neither cat likes me very much, but Odysseus is the one who has perfected lurking in shadows to scare me to death. He loves to bolt out of the dark and screech at me when I take the garbage out the back door for Mom. A lot of the time when I want to watch TV, I have to sit on the floor because Odysseus is flopped across the entire couch and I know if I try to sit next to him, I'll have long, sharp claws embedded in my arm in half a second.

"Shoo, Odysseus," I said halfheartedly. "Go on, get."

He narrowed his eyes and hissed at Meatball and me, showing his needle-sharp teeth and pink tongue. I sighed.

"Sorry, Meatball," I said, scratching the bulldog's head. "We just have to wait until he goes away." I sat down on the top step of the stairs. I didn't have much choice. Once, I tried to chase Odysseus off, and he left little holes in the top of my sneaker where he jabbed at me with his claws. Or if I try to slip past him into my room, he shoots right between my legs, bolts over to the bed, and pees on my comforter before I can stop him. Which, by the way, is *way more gross* than a little drool. It's pretty much the worst thing ever. So usually I figure it's safest to wait until he gets bored and goes away.

But apparently Meatball had had enough of waiting for one day. He trotted straight up to Odysseus and tried to sniff the cat's rear end. I grabbed for his leash to pull him back, thinking Meatball was about to get his big black nose shredded. But instead Odysseus arched his back, all his fur stood on end, and with an angry yowl, the cat fled into Faith's room at the other end of the hall.

"Wow," I said. My admiration for Meatball went way up. If he stuck around, maybe I wouldn't have to spend so much time sitting at the top of the stairs, waiting to get into my own room.

The bulldog sat down and tilted his head at me, like *Well, I* tried *to make friends.* His tongue flopped out of the side of his open mouth. His eyes were all crinkled up in his wrinkles again.

"Good boy, Meatball." I whispered, just in case Mercy or Faith could hear me. He bumped my knees with his head while I opened the door to my room, then barged through ahead of me.

I shut the door, dropped my backpack beside the bed, and turned on my computer, which is always the first thing I do when I get to my room. Meatball snuffled around the edges of the room. Luckily I keep it pretty neat, so there wasn't anything on the floor for him to eat or roll on, although he did manage to knock over a stack of books under my desk.

He also grabbed the gray fleece blanket from the bottom of my bed in his mouth, shook it for a minute, and then dragged it down onto the floor, where he started digging in it with his big paws. I thought about trying to rescue it, but the worst he could do was cover it in dog hair, so I left him to it while I went and filled a bowl of water for him.

It's not a very big room — Mercy and Faith have the bigger bedrooms. I think mine was actually supposed to be an office. There's one window looking onto the backyard and my walls are painted light gray, like the flecks in the mottled beige carpeting. Above the bed and the desk are a couple of *shui-mo* brush paintings of, like, pandas and bamboo and Chinese calligraphy. My mom bought them for me when we visited China a few years ago. I also put up a couple of blown-up photos of me standing on the Great Wall, which was probably the coolest place I've ever been. My sheets are a black-and-white checkerboard pattern and there's one short bookshelf with my books about Houdini and computers. My magic set is stashed on the top shelf of the closet.

But I don't really care what the rest of the room looks like. The important part of the room to me is the big, shiny, black computer sitting on top of my desk. It's all mine and I don't have to share it with anybody. Mercy and Faith share their computer, which is in Mercy's room, but they don't use theirs as much as I use mine. Plus I worked really hard to get my computer — Mom and I made a deal that if I got straight A's in fifth grade, I could choose exactly what I wanted and everything.

I sat down in my black desk chair and opened both my e-mail accounts. I have one for my friends and one I use when I sign up for stuff online, although that last one mostly just gets spam and ads and stuff. I also plugged in my flash drive — I always save my homework and personal projects on it in case I want to work on anything in the school computer lab. Finally I clicked on the Internet to open up all my favorite websites, and then I signed in to chat to see who else was on.

Nikos and Kristal and Jonas were all signed in, as they often are, and so were Pradesh and Danny's little sister, Rosie. For some reason, I ended up on Rosie's list of people she sends funny forwards to. I'm not sure why; Troy and Parker don't get them. Maybe because she sees that I'm online all the time.

Just then Troy's screen name popped up. I clicked on it.

Hey, I wrote. **Guess what?**

Hey Eric, he wrote back. **What?**

Hang on, I'll show you, I typed. I dug my camera out of my desk and swung my chair around. I was surprised to see that Meatball had managed the leap onto my bed when I wasn't paying attention. He was flopped over on his back, sprawled across my comforter, with his eyes closed and his head twisted toward his butt. His big paws stuck straight up in the air like TV antennae.

I snapped a couple of pictures, downloaded them onto my computer, and sent them to Troy.

NO! he wrote almost immediately. **You did not get a dog! :-o**

That's Meatball, I wrote back.

THAT IS SO UNFAIR, he wrote. **Now you all have dogs but me!** He added a frowning face emoticon.

I don't know if we're keeping him, I wrote. **We'll see.**

He's awesome. I WANT ONE.

"Eric!" my mom called from downstairs. "Come set the table!"

Gotta go, I wrote.

:-P, Troy wrote back. **E-mail me l8r.**

When I went to the door, Meatball made a snorting noise and opened one eye to peer at me.

"Stay here, Meatball," I said. "Be good."

Meatball snorted again, as if it was ridiculous to think he wouldn't be, and went back to sleep. It made sense to me that he'd be tired, after his long day of getting abandoned and sitting in the rain and stuff.

I closed my door behind me and saw Odysseus glaring from the doorway of Faith's room. I grinned at him. "Yeah, Odysseus," I said (but quietly, so my sisters wouldn't hear me). "Maybe things are going to change around here."

I was right about that . . . but I had no idea how much.

CHAPTER 4

I was working on my Spanish homework after dinner when there was a knock on my door. I could tell it was Tony because his knock always sounds like *Hey, I hope I'm not disturbing you, you can ignore me if you want . . .* , while Mom's is like, *Look out, here I come!*

"Come in," I called.

Tony slipped inside quickly and shut the door behind him. He once left it open a little too long and Odysseus got in and we spent the rest of the night doing laundry, so now he's really good at getting in and out fast.

"Hey Tony," I said.

Tony starts each day with his hair smoothed down perfectly, and by the end it sticks up in crazy tufts all over the place, like it was now. He has kind of a used-car-salesman smile, but I think he actually means it. He really likes talking to people, strangers especially. It's weird. We're *so* clearly not related.

My actual dad, who lives a few towns away, is quiet like me. Whenever I stay there for a weekend, we mostly spend the whole time on our computers. Sometimes we actually e-mail each other about what we should have for dinner, even if we're just in the next room. It's fine with me. I like being there, because there are no cats plotting my demise.

"HRRUUFFLEWHUFFLE," Meatball snorted, waking up with a start. He sat up on my bed, blinking at Tony.

"Oh, wow," Tony said, grinning from ear to ear. "Wow. Your mom wasn't kidding. That's a bulldog! Man, he's one solid guy. Mind if I pet him?"

"Sure, go ahead," I said. Tony sat down on my bed and rubbed Meatball's back. All the dog's wrinkles smooshed back and forth. Meatball scrunched up his eyes, flopped out his tongue, and beamed at us.

"You're a handsome guy, eh?" Tony said to him. "Bit of a ladies' man, I bet."

"Yeah, ladies who are really into drool and wrinkles," I said.

"So he's just staying for the night?" Tony asked.

"That's the idea," I said. Tony gave me a *hmmm* face.

"That *your* idea?" he asked.

"Well," I said. "I don't know. I mean — do you think Mom would let me keep him?"

"Do you want to?" he said. I have a theory that Tony read in a book somewhere that parents should ask lots of questions, which is why he always answers my questions with other questions.

"Um," I said, spinning my chair in a slow circle. My feet trailed through the carpet. "I guess I don't know yet."

"He seems to like you," Tony said, tugging on Meatball's ear.

"SNAAAAAAARGH," Meatball agreed.

"Yeah, maybe," I said, feeling guilty. "I just kind of thought when we got a dog it'd be, like, a Labrador, or something . . . else."

"I had a Lab growing up," Tony said. "But my girlfriend in high school had a bulldog, and he was great. Really funny, really loyal."

It took me a minute to hear everything he said, because my brain got stuck on "girlfriend in high school." Mom never tells us anything about anything from before we were born. I can't even imagine her in high school. But Tony talks about that stuff all the time, which is kind of cool and also kind of weird.

Luckily there was another knock at my door before I could say anything. Mom came right in and closed the door behind her. She doesn't move as fast as Tony, but the cats never mess with her — perhaps because they remember that she's the one with the needles and the butt thermometer.

Mom was carrying a bowl of water, a couple of washcloths, and a little tub of Vaseline.

"Uh-oh," Tony said. "That looks ominous."

"I'm guessing Meatball hasn't had his wrinkles cleaned in a while," Mom said. "Want to learn how to do it, Eric?"

Um . . . yes? Did I? "OK," I said, because what else could I say?

Tony helped shoo Meatball down onto the carpet and then held his collar while Mom checked the dog's face. He had LOTS of face wrinkles. He kind of ducked his head away from her, rolling his eyes up to give her a pathetic look, but she didn't let him wriggle free. I crouched on the floor beside her and she handed me a washcloth.

"Get that wet," she said. I took the wet cloth and poked it through one of his wrinkles.

Meatball went "SNRRRRRRRRGGGUR-GURGSNARG" in protest and tried to back out of our hands, but Tony held him steady. I went for the next wrinkle, and Meatball managed to twist his head around, clamp his floppy mouth around the corner of the washcloth, and tug it out of my hand. He shook it so it went *whap whap whap* around his face and then he dropped it on the rug and gave me a pleased *well, I took care of THAT, didn't I* expression.

"Sorry, big guy," I said, picking it up and trying again.

It took us about half an hour of wriggling and snorting and flailing and grumbling and washcloth tug-of-war, but finally my mom rubbed a dab of Vaseline on Meatball's nose and said we were done. She gave me a small bite of cheese to give him as a reward, which he devoured at top speed. Then he poked his nose into my hand and peered over it all cross-eyed, trying to find more.

"Good boy," Tony said, patting Meatball's sides. "What a good dog."

"So you just have to do that every day," Mom said. "Oh, and we should clean his teeth every day, too. I mean, we would, if we were going to keep him." She looked at me out of the corner of her eye.

"Um . . . do you think we should?" I asked her. I couldn't decide. I mean, cleaning out Meatball's wrinkles wasn't exactly *fun*. But watching him roll around poking his face into the carpet trying to dry himself off was pretty hilarious. He kept getting too excited and then he'd lose his balance and tumble over and sit up all startled like *Who did that?*

"Well, a dog is a lot of work," Mom said. "You'd have to walk him first thing in the morning and last thing at night. I can't always take care of him for you."

"I could help!" Tony said, and then Mom gave him one of those *that's not how you parent* looks and he was like, "Um, I mean, if you're responsible and . . . show that you're . . . responsible . . . and stuff."

"I could do that," I said. That wasn't the problem. I wanted a dog; I wouldn't mind doing all that for my dog. But I kind of thought I'd get to choose my own dog. Like maybe a dog who could breathe without sounding like his nose was full of giant flaming boogers. But I felt bad thinking that way about poor Meatball. I just didn't know what to do.

"Tell you what," Tony said. "Why don't we hang on to him for a couple of days and see how you feel? If it doesn't work out, we'll find him another home, no problem." He looked at my mom and added quickly, "I mean, if your mom thinks that's a good idea."

"It sounds OK to me," I said. Then at least I wouldn't have to decide right away.

"All right," Mom said, ruffling my hair. "Let me know if you have any questions."

A couple hours later, I discovered Meatball's other superpower. I had just turned off the lights and I was nearly asleep when suddenly . . .

"SNOOOOOOOOOOOOOOOOOOOORRR-RRRRRGGG."

I jolted awake.

"SNOOOOOOOOOOOOOOOOOOOOOO-ORRRRRRRRRRRRRRGGG."

"Oh, man," I said.

"SNNOOOOOOOOOOOOOOOOOOOOOO-OORRRRRRRRRRRRRRRRGGG."

I poked Meatball with my foot. He didn't even wake up. He just rolled over and flopped across my feet with a heavy *whump*. "SNOOOOOOOOOOO-RRRRRRRRRRRRGG," he added helpfully.

I guess I should have expected supersonic snoring, considering the way he breathed when he was awake. I covered my head with my pillow, but it didn't help. The snoring was unbelievable — I was amazed that Mercy and Faith didn't come stomping in to complain. It seemed like the whole house was shaking, although I guess it was probably just my bed.

Eventually I fell asleep somehow. The next morning, Mom woke me up ten minutes early so I could take Meatball outside before breakfast. We don't have a fenced-in yard like Parker's, so I had to put his leash on and follow him around the lawn with a plastic bag. He took way more than ten minutes investigating every inch of our garden (even though he'd given it all a good sniffing the night before, too), so by the time I got inside, I had to scramble so I wouldn't be late to school.

Mercy and Faith get a ride to the high school in the morning with one of their friends from the basketball team. They pointed and laughed at me as I ran down the driveway past them. I ran all the way to the corner where I usually meet Parker, Danny, and Troy, and I was still the last one there. I could see Parker's green backpack and Troy's yellow baseball cap from the top of the street. They were leaning on Mr. Burrell's fence, watching Danny tell a story. I guessed from the way he was jumping and waving his arms that it was a story about his new dog, Buttons.

Parker shook his head when I came panting up. "Your dog's making you late to school, too," he joked. Merlin escaped and followed Parker on the first day of school, and Parker nearly got a detention because he had to take him home. Luckily our new principal is really nice — she even lets him go home during lunch on Wednesdays to let Merlin out. I didn't think my mom would ever let me do something like that, no matter how many good grades I got.

Mom had taken Meatball to work with her. I guess if there's anywhere you can bring a dog to work, it should be a vet's office.

"What dog?" Danny demanded as we started walking. He didn't have his bike with him like he usually did, but he was bouncing a basketball around him as he walked. Danny is the tallest of us, then Parker, then me, and then Troy. Troy is pretty short, but he gets mad if you try to tease him about it — not that that ever stops Danny.

"Eric got a dog, too," Troy said in kind of a grumpy way. I knew he wasn't mad at me, though. It wasn't my fault he didn't have a dog!

"What kind of dog?" Danny wanted to know. "What's his name? Will Buttons like him?"

"Meatball. He's a bulldog," I said. "I don't know — he seemed OK with Merlin."

"Heidi is going to have a heart attack," Parker said. "Don't be surprised if she shows up at your house this afternoon to meet him. She hasn't left Ella's side since Ella got Trumpet." Heidi Tyler is in our class at school, and she *loves* dogs. She's kind of a crazy person about dogs, maybe because she doesn't have one of her own. She's been helping Ella Finegold with her new beagle, Trumpet, but you can tell she's just dying to get her own dog. (And the way you can tell that is she talks about it all the time — way more even than me and Troy put together.)

"Heidi hasn't come over to meet Buttons yet," Danny said.

"Yeah, 'cause you didn't tell anyone about Buttons!" Parker pointed out.

"Well," Danny said, kicking a rock so it bounced into the street. "Buttons isn't so bad. I bet Heidi would like her."

"Ooooooooooo, I think Danny likes Heidi," Troy said with a grin.

Danny shoved him so Troy nearly toppled into the yard we were passing. "You know, *some* guys can just be friends with a girl," he said.

"Yeah, but I bet she'd say yes if you asked her out," Parker offered.

"I don't want to ask her out!" Danny shouted.

"It's OK if you're scared," Parker teased him. "You should talk about your feelings, Danny."

"Man, pick on Eric instead," Danny said, banging the basketball hard against the sidewalk. "He's the one with the real secret crush."

"Hey!" I said. "What'd I ever do to you?" I could feel my cheeks getting warm. I stuck my hands in my jacket pockets and tried to make a face like he was crazy.

"Don't try to hide it," Danny said. "I saw what you did last week."

"I have no idea what you're talking about," I said. "I don't have a crush on anyone."

Troy and Parker started laughing.

"What?" I said. Now I was getting worried. Did they really know?

"Eric," Troy said, fiddling with his glasses like he was in some old movie, "you're dealing with a master detective here. Reading people is what I *do*."

"Sorry, Eric," Parker agreed. "We all know you like her."

"Her *who*?" I said. Maybe they were wrong. Maybe they were thinking of someone else. Maybe they were just joking.

"Well, let's see," Danny said. He pointed at me accusingly, like a lawyer, which is a trick he got from his dad. "The prosecution demands to know: On Friday, when you snuck back into the school with a pink meringue cookie from the bake sale, whose desk did you leave it in?"

Uh-oh.

"Busted!" Troy yelled, laughing again at the look on my face.

"It's OK, Eric," Parker said reassuringly. "Rebekah's cool."

All right, yes. I like Rebekah Waters. But I thought I was hiding it pretty well. It's not like I ever talked about her. And I can't ever think of anything to say to her at school. I get all mumbly and stupid when she talks to me.

A horrible thought struck me. "Do you think *she* knows I like her?" I mean, if it was that obvious to my friends . . . had she figured it out, too?

"No, nuh-uh," Parker said. "No way. I don't think so."

"You don't *think* so?" I stopped and clutched my stomach. "I don't feel good. I think I should go home and hang out with Meatball instead of going to school."

"Eric, don't freak out," Danny said, patting my shoulder. "You never know — maybe she likes you, too."

Yeah, right. I'm not the kind of guy girls notice. Mostly they pay attention to Brett Arbus or Parker or Danny. Danny even went out with Areli Horowitz last year, kind of, for, like, a week. And everyone said Brett had been dating Josephine Clark since the beginning of sixth grade, although it was hard to tell for sure just by looking at them, since Brett is kind of Mr. Charming with all the girls.

Man, I knew buying that cookie for Rebekah was a mistake. What if someone else saw me leave it for her? Someone terrible, like Avery or Natasha and Tara? Or Rebekah herself? Although she looked really surprised when she found it on Monday. And happy, too. So maybe it wasn't all bad. But if she did find out I liked her . . . what would happen then?

"Do you want me to ask her if she likes you?" Troy offered as we started walking again.

"NO!" I nearly yelled. "No, no, no, definitely not. Don't you dare."

"I could find out some other way," Troy suggested. "Like with my detective skills!"

"Yeah, right," I said. "I know what that means. You'd go straight up to one of her friends, like Maggie or Virginia, and ask them if she likes me."

"What's wrong with that?" Troy said, offended. "It'd be like cross-examining the witnesses. How else do you gather evidence?"

"Don't you dare," I said. "Don't any of you do anything. I'll die of embarrassment. I swear." I could see the school up ahead of us. It felt like a magician had made my insides vanish, leaving nothing but terror behind. How could I even look at Rebekah, knowing she might know I liked her?

"Maybe you should just ask her out," Parker suggested.

"I'd rather have my eyes clawed out by my sisters' cats," I said. "You guys better not say anything to anyone."

"We won't," Parker promised with a shrug, and the other two nodded.

I stood at my locker for a minute while they went into class, trying to stop myself from being nervous. Only fifth- and sixth-graders have lockers in our school. I keep mine pretty neat because I usually need to get in and out of it fast. Avery Lafitte's locker is way too close to mine — they're assigned alphabetically — and if he's mad he sometimes shoves or kicks the nearest person for no reason.

Cadence Bly was leaning on Yumi Matsumoto's locker, waiting for her. Cadence had her waist-length black hair clipped up in a big purple barrette that matched her dangly purple hoop earrings. She was wearing a long black skirt and her giant sunglasses with the sparkly rims that she is not supposed to wear in school. She tipped the sunglasses down and peered at me over the top, which is what she does when she's pretending to read someone's mind.

"I sense that you're agitated, Eric," she said in her "spooky" voice, which is really just her regular voice made all quivery and breathy and loony-sounding.

"Nope," I said, taking out my math book. I glanced down the hall, but there was no sign of Avery yet. I checked in the other direction and saw Ella trying to help Heidi shovel stuff back into her locker. Ella threw in a sweater, and Heidi slammed her locker door shut and leaned against it. They were both laughing.

"Your aura is very muddled," Cadence said. She started plucking at the air around my shoulders like she was picking rabbits out of invisible hats. Then she stopped and pushed her sunglasses up on top of her head so she could squint at me. In her normal voice, she said, "Dude, your jacket is *covered* in fur. What have you been rolling in?"

I closed my locker door and brushed at my jacket sleeve. "Nothing," I said. I knew better than to tell Cadence I had a dog. She loves gossip the way Heidi loves dogs or Rosie loves pink. It would be all over the school in half a second, and then what would I do if we decided not to keep him? I'd have to explain it to everyone over and over again.

Cadence squinted at me. "I sense —"

"'Bye Cadence!" I said quickly, and darted into Mr. Peary's classroom. She's in Miss Woodhull's class with Yumi and Troy, so I knew she wouldn't follow me.

Rebekah was already at her desk. Oh, I forgot to mention the worst part. Rebekah's desk is *right next to mine*. So sometimes, if her friend Maggie isn't there yet, she talks to me.

Like this morning.

"Hey Eric," she said with a smile as I sat down. "How's it going?"

Rebekah has soft blond hair and big gray-green eyes. She's left-handed, which I know because sometimes her elbow bumps mine when we're both writing. There are cat stickers on her book covers and notebooks. She likes to wear tights in bright colors like green and purple and blue. Sometimes when she's drawing, she hums TV theme songs, and I don't think she knows she's doing it.

I am a total idiot for liking her. If she wanted to go out with any of the guys in our class, it would probably be Parker or Brett.

"Fine," I mumbled, fiddling with the flash drive in my pocket. See? Even if I did ask her out — which would require, like, hypnotism, by the way — we wouldn't have anything to talk about because of my stupid mumbling problem.

"Oh, shoot," Rebekah said, digging through her desk. "Eric, can I borrow a pencil?"

I lifted my desktop. My seven yellow No. 2 pencils were lined up neatly next to each other. I wondered if that looked super-dorky. I took one out and handed it to her.

"Thanks," she said, smiling again. "I forgot about the math test today."

I nodded. She looked like she was about to say something else, but then Maggie Olmstead threw herself into the seat on the other side of Rebekah and started yammering on about her famous cat's latest cat food commercial.

I relaxed a little, knowing Rebekah wouldn't talk to me again, but my stomach still felt all twisted up. I couldn't wait to get home to Meatball. *He* wouldn't care if I mumbled or couldn't think of anything to say. I figured I could forgive the snoring in exchange for knowing that smushed-up face would never make fun of me for liking Rebekah.

Little did I know there was something much worse coming my way . . . and it would be all Meatball's fault.

CHAPTER 5

I'm usually the first one to get home from school, since Mom and Tony are at work and Mercy and Faith have basketball practice. Most days I find Ariadne on the sofa in front of the TV, her tail swishing back and forth like she's daring me to even *try* sitting down. Odysseus, meanwhile, is posted outside my bedroom door, where he prowls back and forth waiting for it to open so he can go about his evil business.

But that Tuesday, when I came in the kitchen door, I had this weird feeling that something was different. I don't know why; I couldn't see anything unusual in the kitchen. Maybe it was the faint rumbling noise in the background, although I didn't realize what it was at first. There was a note on the table from Mom:

Eric, I brought Meatball back here during lunch. His snoring was disturbing the patients! Please take him for a proper walk when you get home. At least fifteen minutes!

He needs the exercise! And don't forget to take water with you! Love, Mom

Meatball was there? I put the note down, dropped my backpack, and went along the hall into the TV room.

The bulldog was sprawled across the length of the brown leather couch with his whole face buried in the cushions on the back of the sofa. Even so, I could hear his snoring loud and clear. I glanced around the room and spotted Ariadne and Odysseus. The two cats were perched up on the mantelpiece above the fireplace. Their tails were lashing back and forth at the same time and their eyes were narrow slits as they focused the full force of their cat fury on poor oblivious Meatball.

A floorboard creaked under my foot, and Meatball lunged to his paws, scattering couch cushions onto the rug. He blinked, squinting like he was bewildered, lapped his nose with his tongue, and shook his head so his jowls went *flap flap flap*. Then he looked around, and his face lit up in this enormous grin when he saw me. He threw himself off the couch and skidded over to me, crumpling the rug into big wrinkles under his paws. His sturdy body wiggled and bounced with excitement. He bumped my knees with his massive head and tried to stand on his hind legs to knock me over, but I was prepared this time. I hooked my fingers in his collar and wrestled him back to all fours.

"OK, OK, Meatball," I said, secretly pleased. This was much better than the welcome I usually got! "Let's go for a walk."

Oh man, was *that* ever the magic word. Meatball flailed right out of my hands with joy and went sprinting around the TV room making happy grunting noises. His smooshy white paws scrabbled and slipped on the rug, but that didn't stop him from running, beaming, and flapping his tongue at me. He careened off the coffee table and playfully jumped at the cats' tails hanging down from the mantelpiece, earning a pair of hisses. Every time he hit the floor there was a *thud* and the house trembled.

Ariadne gave me a cold look, like she was thinking *I know that* you *brought this menace into my house. Don't think I'll forget it.*

I tried to rearrange the room while Meatball cavorted around my feet. I put all the cushions back and refolded the orange-and-white throw blankets that Meatball had dug into a perfect nest for himself. I straightened the coffee table and the rug. I could feel the cats staring at me the whole time, and I felt like I could hear my sisters' voices in my head, complaining about the mess that Meatball had made. There were a couple of damp drool spots on the pillows that I rubbed at, hoping they would fade before everyone got home.

I also used a lint roller on the couch — we have one that Mercy and Faith are supposed to use for the cat hair, but they almost never do. It's like a rolling pin of sticky tape that picks up fur from cushions. It worked pretty well, actually, but boy was there a lot of fur on the couch. (And not all of it was Meatball's, in case you were wondering.)

"Come on, Meatball," I said finally, heading back to the kitchen. Mom had left me a special water bottle for dogs. You can hang it around your neck and it has a dish attached to it, so you don't have to carry a bunch of things in your hands. I filled the bottle and put it on. Meatball's leash was coiled on the counter by the back door. It took me a while to get him to calm down enough so I could lift up his wrinkles and clip the leash to his collar. While I was doing that, the phone rang, but my arms were full of bulldog, so I let the answering machine pick up.

"Hey Mercy, hey Faith. It's George," a boy's voice said. "Coach said I should talk to you about the rally next week, so, like, call me back, OK?" He left his number and hung up. I was surprised. I didn't know Mercy and Faith talked to anyone, especially boys.

Finally I got Meatball's leash attached and we headed out the door into the sunshine.

It was the last day of September, and a few of the leaves were starting to turn yellow. Meatball stopped at the bottom of the driveway and shook himself from tip to tail, then took a deep breath. I did the same thing (the deep breath, not the shaking — how weird would that look?!). It smelled like fall, all clean and windy and apple cider-y.

Meatball decided to go left from our driveway, which was fine with me. Our neighborhood is pretty quiet, so we could walk anywhere. I wondered if we should go over to Parker's house and see Merlin. Or to Danny's to see Buttons.

But I kind of liked being out with Meatball, walking my own dog by myself. It felt sort of grown-up and cool. I figured I would let Meatball decide where he wanted to go.

Boy, was *that* a big mistake.

He snortled cheerfully along the street, sniffing every fence post and tree and fire hydrant that we went by. A couple of my neighbors waved at us from their yards. At the end of the block, Meatball decided to go right, across the street, instead of left toward Parker's. Soon he turned right again, and we started climbing uphill, past houses that were a little bigger than mine. There were a lot of big trees shading the street here, so we had to stop every thirty seconds for an extended sniffing session. I didn't mind. I was relieved that I didn't have to make conversation with anyone. I could just walk in peace and think about the websites I was building and computer problems I was trying to solve.

After a few blocks, Meatball stopped in front of a light gray house with purple shutters. A front porch wrapped around the outside and there was a round tower with one of those big curved windows on the second floor. Meatball practically shoved his face through the slats of the white picket fence, inhaling vigorously.

I stood there while he snuffled, looking at the big flower bushes around the porch. They had enormous purple-and-blue clusters of flowers on them and big dark green leaves. My eyes drifted to the driveway beside the fence, where a dark blue hybrid car sat next to a bicycle that was propped against the house. The car had a couple of political and environmental bumper stickers on it. I squinted at it. Had I seen that car before? At school, maybe?

Then I noticed that the bike was a girl's bike. It was light purple with a white basket on the front. And all over the basket were . . . cat stickers.

This was Rebekah's house!

I panicked. What would she think if she looked outside and saw me standing there? Would she think I was some kind of weirdo stalker?

I nearly dropped Meatball's leash and ran away up the street, but of course I couldn't do that. Instead I said, "Let's go, Meatball!" and started walking as fast as I could.

My arm was practically yanked out of its socket as I reached the end of the leash. I turned around.

Meatball had planted himself on the sidewalk in front of Rebekah's house. I mean, it was like he'd grown roots right there, like a big old oak tree that was never going to move. His paws were braced against the concrete. His shoulders were hunched. His face was stubborn. He was leaning his whole weight back against the end of the leash, and he wasn't going anywhere.

I was in big trouble.

CHAPTER 6

Meatball, come *on*," I said desperately, yanking on the leash. Rebekah could come outside at any minute! She might even be inside watching me right that second. In which case, she was probably thinking *What kind of idiot can't even walk his own dog?*

I leaned all my weight into pulling him, but he just wrinkled his forehead in this worried way, like *Are you feeling all right? Do you want to sit down and relax for a minute?* I definitely did not want to relax. I wanted to get out of there as fast as possible.

"Meatball! Come here! Come on!" I said, beckoning. He picked up one front paw, sniffed it all over with a studious expression, and then slowly lowered himself until he was lying down right there on the sidewalk.

Another dog started barking somewhere nearby, a high yapping noise. Meatball's ears twitched curiously, but his head stayed flopped on the ground. I glanced at Rebekah's house. Did I see the white curtains moving in the downstairs window? Was someone looking out at us?

I tried dragging Meatball again, but he sat up and braced his paws, scrabbling and shoving himself backward. Now I was sure I saw movement behind the windows. Someone was coming! Probably Rebekah! I was doomed!

Frantically I searched through my pockets. Did I have anything that would get him to move?

I felt my keys, the plastic bag, my flash drive, and my library card. Then a shock ran through me as my fingers felt something hard and crumbly. The dog biscuits from the waiting room! I'd only given Meatball one of them the day before.

I pulled out the last biscuit and waved it in the air. "Hey Meatball," I said. "What's this? Huh? Something you want?"

His little floppy ears flicked forward. His forehead wrinkles went up. He leaned toward me, sniffing the air. He leaned closer . . . and closer . . . I waved the biscuit just out of his reach, then took a step backward.

Meatball surged to his feet and lunged at the biscuit. I pulled it back just in time. I'm sure if he'd snarfed it out of my hand, he'd have gone right back to sitting. But instead he trotted after me, his eyes fixed on the treat in my hand. I led him a few paces away from Rebekah's gate, and then I turned to start running.

Rebekah's front door was swinging open!

I bolted, and luckily Meatball sprinted along with me. I guess he was like *OK, anything for a biscuit!*

I thought I heard Rebekah's voice say: "Eric?" as I shot past the tall bushes at the end of her yard, but I didn't stop running until we reached the next block and turned down a new street, well out of view of her house. Then I stopped with my hands on my knees, panting. Meatball was panting even harder than me, but he came up and shoved his big flat head against my hand, demanding his treat.

"You so don't deserve this," I said to him, but I broke it into small pieces and let him gobble it up.

I felt like the world's biggest moron. If that really had been Rebekah coming outside, what was she thinking now? That I lurked around her house and then ran away when she saw me? She must have thought I was such a weirdo.

"Thanks a *lot*, Meatball," I said. He snorted and leaned against my leg, beaming in his cheerful goofy way.

My whole face was hot with embarrassment. The scene kept playing again and again in my head as we walked home. It was too easy to imagine Rebekah glancing out her window and being like, "Is that Eric? Why is he just standing around in front of my house? Oh wow, I bet he likes me. He's such a freak! And his dog is funny-looking, too." She probably didn't even like dogs, since she liked cats so much.

At least no one was home yet when we got back. The cats were lounging on the couch again. They both raised their heads as we came up to the den. Their tails flicked silently as they stared at me. The message was pretty clear: *Don't you dare come in here.*

Unfortunately for them, Meatball isn't much of a mind reader. He flew into the room and launched himself onto the couch with reckless glee. I guess he figured everyone should be as happy to see him as he was to see them.

Ariadne and Odysseus fled with yowls of fury. They bolted past me — not even stopping to claw my legs or anything — and shot up the stairs. From the couch, Meatball cocked his head at me like *Jeez, I know I smell, but is it that bad?*

"Wow," I said. "You know what this means, Meatball? It means we can watch TV. You know when the last time I watched TV in the afternoon was? Pretty much never."

He stuck out his tongue and slurped at his nose. I wrestled him over onto the next cushion and sat down. Normally I hang out in my room when I'm home alone, hiding from the cats. It was weird to have the living room to myself. Well, myself and Meatball. He turned in a circle, knocking cushions off the couch, and finally lay down with his big chin on my knee.

I couldn't have concentrated on my homework anyway. I'd already started the "interview an Egyptian pharaoh" essay that was due on Friday. I had written the first half at school and saved it on my flash drive. What I needed was to stop thinking about Rebekah's house. I flipped channels until I found a *Battlestar Galactica* marathon. Meatball immediately fell asleep. It was lucky I'd already seen these episodes, because his snoring made it impossible to hear half of what was going on.

Mercy and Faith got home an hour later. I heard them come in the kitchen door, already making the kissy noises they make for their cats. But Ariadne and Odysseus didn't come downstairs, probably because they were sulking.

My sisters stopped in the doorway of the living room and narrowed their eyes at me and Meatball. Today they were wearing sweater sets — turquoise for Mercy, forest green for Faith. Their hair was wet from showering after basketball practice. They looked at Meatball like he was a fungus growing on the couch.

"Where's Ariadne?" Mercy asked.

"And Odysseus?" Faith demanded.

I shrugged. "Upstairs, I think. It's a big house."

Mercy's icy gaze darted around the room and then returned to Meatball. "They're *usually* in *here*," she said.

"I know," I said, and added innocently, "I guess they didn't want to watch TV with us."

Faith put her hands on her hips. "We have to watch a DVD for school."

"OK," I said, although I was pretty sure she was lying. I started to get up, but Meatball's head was like a bowling ball in my lap. He sleep-snorted and wriggled farther onto my lap, like he was pinning me down.

"Um," I said. "You know what? This episode will be done in twenty minutes. OK?"

Mercy and Faith looked as outraged as their cats. I guess I don't say no to them very often. Their mouths opened and closed.

Quickly I added, "Hey, did you hear the message on the machine for you? Some guy named George."

That got their attention.

"George?" Faith said.

"George Marvell?" Mercy demanded.

I shrugged. "I don't know. Something about a rally."

"I'll call him back," Faith said, jumping toward the stairs.

"No, *I'll* call him back!" Mercy shouted, chasing after her. They both thundered up the stairs like a herd of girl buffalo racing to get to the cutest boy buffalo.

"Why aren't girls falling all over themselves to call *me*, huh, Meatball?" I asked, scratching the wrinkles on his head. He opened his eyes a crack, gave me a look like there was no hope for me, and fell asleep again.

I imagined calling poor George to warn him about my sisters. That would definitely get me smothered in my sleep.

Tony got home next. He came into the living room, jingling his keys in his pocket, and squinted at the TV.

"Hey Eric," he said. "Whatcha watching? This looks serious. Are you allowed to watch that?" Tony is still working on sounding like a dad. Mostly he sounds like a TV version of a dad, but I know he's trying.

"I've seen these episodes before with Mom," I said. "She said I could watch them as long as she watched them, too, in case she needed to talk to me about anything." I have to say, I think it's pretty cool to have a mom who'll watch *Battlestar Galactica* with me, although I wouldn't tell the guys about that.

"Oh," Tony said. "OK. Um. Did you do your homework?"

See what I mean? "I don't have much," I said. "I'll finish it after dinner."

Tony nodded, but I could see that he was wondering whether to tell me I should do it now.

"I figured I'd hang out on the couch with Meatball for a bit," I explained.

"Oh, yeah, sure," Tony said, smiling at the dog. "Can I watch the news when this is over?"

"Sure," I said. He came in and sat on the other side of Meatball, which was kind of funny because he had to squish himself in between Meatball's giant butt and the end of the sofa. He rubbed Meatball's belly, and the dog rolled over to let him, without really waking up.

"Anything new in school?" Tony asked during the next commercial break. "How's your new teacher?"

"Mr. Peary is cool," I said. "He's kind of obsessed with Leonardo da Vinci." Mr. Peary had been sneaking in da Vinci stuff slowly since the first day. There was a poster of a da Vinci drawing on the wall behind Mr. Peary's desk. His mug had a little flying machine designed by Leonardo printed on the side. We weren't even studying the Renaissance yet — we were still learning about Ancient Egypt — but Mr. Peary kept bringing up da Vinci anyway, and he got this shiny look in his eyes whenever he mentioned him. It was kind of funny. From the way Mr. Peary talked about him, it sounded like Leonardo da Vinci would be everyone's hero by the end of the semester.

"What about your friends?" Tony asked. "Any of you have a girlfriend yet?" He gave me his big-toothed smile. He's always teasing Parker about being a ladies' man, because girls talk to Parker all the time, although as far as I know Parker isn't interested like that in any of the girls in our class.

"No, no, no," I said. "No way. Nuh-uh."

"You sound very sure about that," Tony said, grinning.

"Oh, look, the episode's over," I said. "Time to do my homework." I passed him the remote and woke the slumbering beast on top of me. Meatball sat up and let Tony scratch his head for a second, and then he followed me up the stairs to my room.

The cats were lurking down the hall by Faith's room, but they didn't come any closer as I slipped through my door. Meatball rolled on the carpet for a minute, snorting enthusiastically, and then wriggled himself under the bed until only his butt and little fat tail were sticking out. Soon I could hear his snores shaking my bed.

I turned on my computer and found a bunch of messages from Parker and Danny and Troy, wondering where I was. Parker was still signed in to chat, so I wrote to him.

I'm home, I typed. **Why? Is something happening?**

Where were you? Parker wrote. **You're always online!**

Walking Meatball, I wrote back. **And watching TV downstairs. I'm not ALWAYS online!**

Yeah, OK, whatever, he said.

Something pinged in the background. I was getting a message from someone called "Maltizu." That didn't sound familiar. I clicked on it.

The message said, **Hi Eric!** So it was someone who knew me.

Hi, I wrote. **Who's this?**

It's Rebekah!

My heart plummeted into my shoes. *Oh, man. Oh, man.* Why was she writing to me all of a sudden? I stared at the screen. I had no idea what to say to her. The cursor flashed for a moment. And then a new message popped up.

Hey, did I see you outside my house today?

CHAPTER 7

I panicked. Listen, I'm not brave like Harry Houdini. I'm not cool like Parker. I'm just Eric. I do not casually chat with girls like Rebekah every day. I know, I sound like such a coward. But what would you have done?

Me, I did the stupid scaredy-cat thing. I hit the power switch on my computer and jumped away from it. And I know better; I know how you're supposed to shut down a computer properly. But I kind of freaked out. My computer went *EEEERRrrrruuuu* and the screen went black.

I sat down on the floor and buried my head in my hands. Meatball crawled out from under the bed and gave me a puzzled look with his forehead all wrinkled up.

"This is all your fault," I said to him. "You are a very bad dog."

He tilted his head one way and then the other. And then he decided that what I needed was to have my face licked off.

"ACK, STOP!" I yelped. "Meatball! OFF!" I braced my hands against his broad shoulders and tried to hold him back, but he threw his whole body at my face with a very determined expression. His head mushed up into the fat wrinkles around his neck and his giant pink scratchy tongue went *SLURP SLURP* along my cheek until I gave up and fell over backward, laughing.

Pleased, he sat on my chest and beamed down at me.

"You're not forgiven," I said. "We might not even keep you, you know. You should try to be less of a pain."

In response, Meatball drooled on my T-shirt.

I didn't turn on my computer again for the rest of the night. Finally Parker called to see if I was OK. I told him I was having computer trouble, but I don't think he believed me. It was a pretty new computer, and he knew I'd be freaking out more if there was anything wrong with it. I wasn't going to tell him about Rebekah, though. I was embarrassed enough.

I felt more and more nervous thinking about school the next day. What would I say to her when she asked me in person? When I woke up in the morning, it was like lots of tiny Meatballs were banging around in my stomach, crashing into the walls and scrabbling through my insides.

Mom was in the kitchen drinking coffee when I came downstairs with Meatball. Faith was burning toast in the toaster. She likes it that way for some reason.

As I put on my shoes to take Meatball out, I said, "Mom, I'm not feeling so great. Could I maybe stay home today?"

"Oh, what*ever*," Faith said, rolling her eyes.

Mom frowned and felt my forehead. "You feel normal." Mom's vet side always comes out when I'm sick. I half expect her to hide my medicine inside a dog treat one day without noticing.

"It's my stomach," I said, and I wasn't even exaggerating. Every time I thought of Rebekah, I felt really queasy.

"Big faker," said Faith. She grabbed the raspberry jam from the fridge and stuck out her tongue at me behind Mom's back.

"Well," Mom said, tapping her chin, "all right, but I can't stay home with you. I have too many appointments. Do you want me to see if Tony is free? Or your dad?"

"No, I'll be OK by myself," I said, relieved. That's the upside of being a good kid. Mom would never have believed Mercy or Faith if they wanted to stay home sick, because they try it all the time to get out of big tests and stuff. I'd never done this before — I usually go to school even when I am actually sick. (OK, I'll admit it: I don't like being home alone all day with Ariadne and Odysseus.) So she figured I must be serious.

"I'll leave Meatball with you, then," she said. "Call me or Tony if you need anything."

"He just wants to stay home with that stupid drooling dog," Faith said.

"Faith, leave your brother alone," Mom said absentmindedly, picking up the newspaper.

I ducked out the door before Faith could suck me into an argument. Meatball and I wandered around the yard for a bit, and then we went back up to my room and waited until everyone was gone.

I knew I couldn't hide at home forever. But maybe by tomorrow Rebekah would forget about seeing me at her house.

After nine o'clock, I figured it was safe to turn on my computer again. Everyone I knew would be at school. There was no chance of Rebekah chatting with me now.

I clicked through a few more e-mails from Danny and Troy and checked my favorite websites, but there was nothing interesting. I didn't even feel like watching TV. I just wanted sixth grade to be over.

Meatball nosed his way under my desk and lay down on my feet, grunting.

"What should we do?" I asked him. "We could go scare off the cats again. That was fun."

Snort, Meatball offered, closing his eyes. His floppy jowls were all pooched up on the carpet.

"OK," I said. "I guess I'll finish my essay." I leaned over in my chair, trying not to disturb Meatball, and grabbed my jacket from the bottom of the bed. I rummaged in the pocket for my flash drive.

"That's weird," I said, turning the pocket inside out. I felt in the other one. I checked my pants pockets from the day before. I emptied out my backpack and searched through the whole thing. Then I checked my jacket again.

Finally it hit me.

My flash drive was gone.

This was a disaster. It wasn't just that I'd lost the first half of my essay and would have to start over. If anyone found the flash drive, they'd have all my homework from the last month and a bunch of personal things, too — notes about my Houdini website and magic tricks and ideas I'd had for birthday presents for my friends and photos of Merlin and even this dumb video of me doing a magic trick that I'd had Troy record for me. I mean, I write practically everything down in my computer somewhere, and then I back it all up on the drive. That's what you're supposed to do — but you're not supposed to lose the drive afterward!

Just in case, I checked the pockets of everything I'd worn in the last week. It was nowhere. I tried to think. What had I done with it? Meatball was watching me with this placid, unworried expression.

"Oh, sure," I said. "It's not *your* life that could be out there for anyone to find."

He slurped his big pink tongue over his nose and closed his eyes, going *smack smack smack* with his mouth.

"You didn't —" I said. "No, you wouldn't — would you?"

Could Meatball have *eaten* my flash drive?

I knelt down beside him and lifted his drooping jowls to look at his teeth. He opened his eyes, startled, and let out a woof of surprise. His expression was so indignant and innocent that I almost believed he knew what I was accusing him of. His breath smelled like dog biscuits.

Suddenly I remembered when I'd last had the drive. I had felt it in my pocket outside of Rebekah's house.

"This *is* your fault!" I cried, poking Meatball in the side. "It must have fallen out while we were running away."

I jumped to my feet and Meatball scrambled to his paws too. His tongue flopped out and the corners of his mouth turned up as he grinned and wheezed.

"Man, I hope Rebekah didn't find it," I said, rubbing my head. I didn't *think* there was anything on there about her . . . but what if there was? Plus then she'd definitely know it had been me outside her house. "We'd better go look for it now, while she's at school."

Meatball did an excited wriggle-dance that started with his butt and ended with his front paws flying up and then landing in a play bow.

"I should leave you behind," I said sternly. I checked my watch. It was nearly ten a.m. There was no way Rebekah would be home; probably no one would be there. But it would look much weirder if I was lurking around her house *without* a dog. Just to be safe, I had to take Meatball.

"OK, but don't be an idiot this time," I said, leading him downstairs. He snorted and cavorted around the kitchen for a while until I got his leash on. I could see Odysseus's black tail lashing from a high shelf in the pantry. Ariadne was probably busy digging a tunnel to my room to exact her revenge.

I checked all around the back door first, which was tough because Meatball was raring to go. He pretty much dragged me all the way down the driveway, plowing ahead with his strong, sturdy legs. I leaned back and stared at the ground on either side of me, but I didn't see my flash drive anywhere.

Meatball wanted to go the same way we'd gone the day before, and we had an enormous struggle at the bottom of the driveway as I tried to drag him one way and he tried to drag me the other. But finally I got him walking along the path we'd taken home from Rebekah's. Once we were moving, it was easier to look for the flash drive, because once again Meatball had to stop and sniff everything.

Not when we got to the top of Rebekah's block, though. I was kicking a few leaves aside, checking underneath them, when all of a sudden Meatball's ears twitched forward. His big nose went *SNIIIIIIIIIIIIIIIFF!* And then he bolted down the street toward Rebekah's. I mean, I had no idea a fat dog like that could move so fast. The leash flew out of my hands before I realized he was moving, and then he was just a blur of brown and white charging along the sidewalk, stubby legs pumping madly.

"Meatball!" I called. "Sit! Stay! STOP!" Of course, we hadn't learned "sit" yet, or anything that a normal dog like Merlin could do. I raced after Meatball.

He skidded to a stop outside Rebekah's house and mashed his face into the slats of the fence. It was like he was hoping he could press himself through the tiny gap if he just pushed hard enough and wanted it badly enough. He pawed at the fence and let out a little whine. I caught up to him, gasping for breath.

"What is wrong with you?" I demanded. "Why are you such a crazy dog? What is your obsession with this house?"

He sat down and leaned into the fence, giving the yard beyond a mournful, big-eyed look, as if it was his long-lost mother and he'd finally found her after years of searching.

I looked from Meatball to the house and back. "Meatball — this isn't *your* house, is it?"

Meatball snorted, but that was his answer to everything. Well, I wasn't about to ring the doorbell to find out. Maybe I'd tell my mom and see what she thought.

In the meantime, I had to find my flash drive.

I tied Meatball's leash to the fence, although he sure didn't seem like he wanted to go anywhere, and then I walked slowly up and down the sidewalk, studying every inch of it. Leaves, twigs, two pennies, a silver gum wrapper . . . but no flash drive. I noticed a drain in the gutter next to the sidewalk. Could it have fallen in there? I crouched down to look more closely.

Meatball let out a little whine.

"It's OK," I said over my shoulder, poking a stick through the holes. I thought I saw something reflected down there. "We'll be done in a second."

"Looking for this?" said a familiar voice.

I froze. *It can't be.* I turned around slowly.

Rebekah was standing on the other side of the fence, holding up my flash drive.

CHAPTER 8

But —" I sputtered. "But — you — what — but school!" I know. I was a conversational genius. This is what happens to my brain when I'm around Rebekah.

"You're supposed to be in school too!" she said. She was smiling. She didn't look like she hated me for being a weirdo stalker lurking around her house.

"I . . . um . . . I mean, I'm . . . um, sick," I said lamely.

"That's too bad. I have a dentist appointment," she said. "In an hour. Mom said I could stay home for the morning. Hopefully I don't need braces." No way did Rebekah need braces. Her teeth were perfect. "Cross your fingers for me!" she added. She crossed the fingers of the hand that wasn't holding my flash drive. Then she noticed me looking at it.

"Oh, here," she said, handing it over. "So it *was* you out here yesterday, right?"

"Uh," I said, wondering if I could disappear into the drain behind me. "Oh — yeah. I mean, uh . . ." I pointed at Meatball.

"Were you saying hello?" she said to the dog, leaning over the fence to scratch Meatball's head. "Yeah, I've seen you using that flash drive at the computer lab, so I figured it was you I saw. Don't worry, I didn't look at the files." I shoved it in my pocket with a relieved sigh.

"Thanks," I said.

"Why?" she added, smiling mischievously. "Are there big dark secrets on there?"

"No!" I blurted. "No, no, no."

"You do that a lot," she said, leaning on the fence. "When you say "no," you say it three times. Like you're casting a spell on people so they'll believe you. I mean, in the books I read, three is always the magic number, so that's what it seems like to me."

I didn't know I did that. "What books?" I said, and then felt like the bravest person alive. I'd asked Rebekah Waters a question!

"I like fantasy stories," she said. "With magic and stuff. I'll read anything by Diana Wynne Jones. And I love the Prydain Chronicles and *The Dark Is Rising* and oh my gosh, don't get me started. So this is your dog? I didn't know you had a dog."

Meatball was straining at his leash to get to her, scrabbling at the wood of the fence. I saw with horror that he'd left a few claw marks in the white paint. His tongue was flopped out the side of his mouth and he was going *gaaarrrrghhhaaaarrrraagggaarrrrh* in a desperate, lovelorn way. I kind of wished I could say I had no idea where he'd come from, but of course I couldn't.

"Yeah," I said. "Sort of. I mean . . . sort of. He, um . . . he was abandoned . . . like, at my mom's office." I looked at her sideways to see if she'd react. It couldn't have been her family who abandoned him, right? Rebekah would never do that to a dog. And she didn't act like she'd ever seen him before.

"Aww, he's so cute," Rebekah said, rubbing the wrinkles on the top of his head. "What a big goofball." Meatball wriggled delightedly and licked her hand. *SLURP!*

Fantastic, I thought. *Just what every girl wants. A big drooling dog slobbering all over her hands. Especially when she's a cat person and doesn't like dogs at all.*

But Rebekah just laughed and wiped her hand on her jeans. "I think he likes me."

"He loves your house," I said, finally getting through a whole sentence without any "um"s. "I thought . . . I mean, I wondered if . . . maybe he lived here . . . um, before."

Rebekah shook her head. "Not while we've been here, which is years. Oh!" Her eyes lit up. "I bet I know why! Stay here. I mean — come in, come into the yard." She beckoned with both hands, unlatching the front gate. I untied Meatball and he barreled right inside, snorting delightedly. His whole body vibrated as he snuffled across the grass.

I couldn't believe it. I was standing in Rebekah's yard.

"OK, wait here," she said. She closed the gate, turned, and ran up the stairs of the porch. I practically had to tackle Meatball and sit on him to keep him from following her. By the time she came back, I had grass stains all over my jeans and leaves in my hair. But she didn't seem to notice.

She was carrying something small and furry over one shoulder, with her arms wrapped around it. Behind her I saw her dad come to the door and wave at me. I waved back and he disappeared inside again.

Rebekah sat down on the grass beside me. "This is Noodles," she said, and I realized what she was holding was a tiny dog. It was mostly white with some brown patches, like Meatball, but that was the only way they were alike. This dog was fluffy all over and almost as small as Buttons, Danny's poodle puppy. She had furry, floppy ears and a tiny black nose and a little pink tongue that was maybe a tenth the size of Meatball's slobbery tongue.

"You have a dog!" I said, surprised.

"We just got her. Isn't she awesome?" Rebekah said, ruffling Noodles's fur.

"I thought — uh, I thought you liked cats," I said. I felt like an idiot as soon as I said it. *Not that I stare at your notebook all the time or anything. Not that I've noticed the cat stickers on your locker because I'm such a stalker.*

"I like cats *and* dogs," Rebekah said. "Doesn't everyone? It's like liking ice cream *and* cookies. They're both great. We have two cats — they're around somewhere. But Noodles is our first dog."

Rebekah put her dog down on the grass and Noodles shook herself so all her fur went *poof* around her little face. Then she looked up at Meatball, blinked her round black eyes, and wagged her fluffy little tail.

Meatball seriously just about had a heart attack. His butt started wagging and he bounced right up in the air on all fours and shoved his face into the grass and wriggled in a circle and fell over on his side and rolled and flailed his paws and wobbled back up again with this ecstatic expression. The whole time he was snort-breathing, which sounded kind of like growling and panting and snuffling at the same time, *aahhhhrrrrff hrrfff haahaahaaah hrrrrff haahaah snnrrsnrrrsnrrrr* . . . kind of like that. It sounded *really* weird and a little crazy. I kept thinking *Man, Rebekah must think my dog is such a freak.* My face felt like it was on fire.

Finally he dropped into a play bow with his front paws splayed out to either side, his head resting on the ground, and his butt up in the air. A corner of his tongue peeked out of his mouth and all the wrinkles in his forehead were scrunched up like he was saying *Please like me! Please please please like me!*

The littler dog jumped back when he first started thrashing around, but once he was still, she took a couple steps toward him, stretching out her nose. Meatball stayed in his play bow, but I could see he was vibrating with excitement. Noodles sniffed his face cautiously. Then she tried to go around him to sniff his butt, but that was too much excitement for Meatball, who started bouncing and rolling again. Noodles sat down and yipped sternly at him.

"Sorry," I said. "Meatball is kind of a spaz."

"Meatball and Noodles!" Rebekah said. "That's so cute! It's like they were destined for each other. Man, he *loves* her!" Meatball threw himself onto his back with all four paws in the air. His eyes rolled sideways as he tried to watch Noodles, who was tentatively sniffing around him again.

"What, uh, what kind of dog is she?" I asked.

"She's a Maltese–shih tzu mix," Rebekah said. "At least that's what we think. We rescued her from a shelter a few months ago, so they were just guessing that she might be a Maltizu."

A light went on in my head. "Maltizu!" I said. "That's your screen name."

"Yeah," she said, ruffling the fur on Noodles's head. "Hey, what happened while we were chatting last night?"

"Uh," I said. "Um — my computer — froze."

"Oh, ours does that all the time," Rebekah said, like she *totally believed me*!

"Rebekah!" her dad called from the door. "We have to go soon."

"OK!" she called back. "Sorry, Meatball," she said, rubbing his belly. "Noodles has to go back inside."

"Ooooorrrrrrr," Meatball protested mournfully as Rebekah scooped up Noodles in her arms. He poked her jeans with his flat nose, squishing up the wrinkles around his mouth. Rebekah patted him on the head, which was all the encouragement he needed.

Meatball reared up on his back legs and planted his front legs on her waist like he was thinking about climbing her to get to Noodles. His big slobbery tongue went *SLURP SLURP* along her bare arm.

"Oof!" Rebekah said with surprise, staggering back a pace at the weight of all that bulldog resting on her. I was mortified. *She must think he's an uncontrollable beast.* I jumped up and grabbed Meatball's collar, wrestling him off her.

"Sorry!" I said. "Sorry, sorry."

"You did it again," she said, smiling. "Magic power of three. Don't worry, Meatball. You'll see Noodles again soon."

"Rebekah!" her dad called again from the house.

"Coming! See you tomorrow, Eric. Feel better!" Rebekah said with a little wave. She ran back up the porch steps. I saw her set Noodles down in the front hall before the door closed.

Meatball was not going to let the small fluffy dog of his dreams go that easily. He lunged toward the porch and I had to get down on my knees and literally wrap my arms around his big shoulders to hold him back. He scrabbled and flailed and tried to distract me by licking off my face, but finally he sat down, tipped his head up to the sky, and went, "Aaaoooorrrooo!"

And then, of course, *snort snort snort.*

"We're going home," I said to him. "You've caused enough trouble for one day."

His tongue rolled out of his mouth as he grinned at me. It went *flap flap flap* up and down like a sail whapping around in a high breeze. He looked extremely pleased with himself. We only have one guy in our class who has had more than one girlfriend ever, and that's Brett. He always has this look like he's the coolest guy in town and of course everyone loves him. That was the kind of expression Meatball had on his face right about then.

"Well, I'm glad *you're* so happy," I said. "You made me look like an idiot."

Meatball practically shrugged. His face was like *Oh, you don't need any help from me in that department.*

"Yeah, thanks," I said, wrapping his leash around my hand and tugging him out the gate. He followed reluctantly, digging his paws into the grass and casting woebegone looks over his shoulder at Rebekah's house.

It took so long just to drag him onto the sidewalk that we were still there when Rebekah and her dad came out the side door and got into the car. I wanted to jump into one of the giant flower bushes and hide.

Seriously, what kind of incompetent dork can't even walk his own dog?

Rebekah waved from the front seat as they drove by. I think she was laughing. I'm pretty sure she was laughing at me. It was the most embarrassing thing ever.

But as I finally got Meatball walking down the street again, one thing Rebekah had said popped up in my head.

Don't worry, Meatball. You'll see Noodles again soon.

Did she mean that? Did that mean she wanted Meatball to visit again?

And maybe . . . me?

CHAPTER 9

If I hadn't been so focused on worrying about Rebekah, I probably would have suspected what was coming. I mean, my sisters and their cats were the bosses of the house, even if Mom and Tony didn't realize how often they got everything they wanted. And they weren't going to let anything change that. Especially not a big snorting pile of overenthusiastic fur and drool like poor Meatball.

They launched their attack at dinner that night. For once, we were all at the table at the same time, without any guests (like Parker, who comes over a lot, especially when his sister is making strange tofu things). Meatball was shut up in my room, snoring with his head buried under my pillows. Ariadne and Odysseus were prowling back and forth under the dinner table, and I had my feet tucked up under my chair, hoping they wouldn't suddenly attack from below. Tony had made fried chicken and baked potatoes and asparagus. He had lived on his own for a long time before he met Mom, so he's actually a pretty good cook.

"Mom," Mercy said in her "sweet" voice. I looked up sharply. I know that voice. It's the *we need new basketball sneakers more than Eric needs a new computer mouse* voice. Also the *you should teach us how to drive this afternoon instead of taking Eric for his long-overdue haircut like you promised* voice.

Mercy is better at the voice than Faith is, so she's always the one to start it off. Faith has trouble even pretending to be that nice, so mostly she says "Yeah, Mom" and "Exactly!" while Mercy talks. I think it's crazy how Mom can't spot their act coming from a mile away. But it always works on her, every single time.

"Yes, dear?" Mom said, cutting her asparagus into neat bite-sized pieces.

Mercy tossed her hair back and gave Mom a smile that said *I know it's silly of me to even ask this, but* . . . . "Faith and I were just wondering when that dog is going to the shelter."

"Yeah," Faith chimed in.

"Oh," Mom said, glancing at me. "Well . . ."

"I really think he's upsetting Ariadne," Mercy said, practically batting her eyelashes. "She's been meowing a lot more for the last couple of days.

Yesterday I found her hiding under my bed when I came home. I don't know what that dog did to her while we were out, but she was, like, totally *traumatized*."

Yeah. I bet. Ariadne is about as easy to traumatize as Godzilla.

"Exactly!" Faith said. "I think Odysseus is losing his fur, he's so nervous."

I nearly spit baked potato all over the table. Odysseus was many things — sinister, conniving, vengeful, bullying, surprisingly full of pee — but he was never, ever nervous.

"The sooner we get rid of that dog, the better," Mercy said. "Right, Mom? I mean, he's so not us. The couch was, like, *covered* in dog fur last night."

I wondered how she could tell through all the cat fur that's usually all over it. Plus I'd used the lint roller on it again, so it wasn't even that bad.

"Yeah," Faith said. "It was totally gross."

You know what's gross? Cat pee. *Nothing* is grosser than cat pee.

"Oh," my mom said. "But — it's so nice for Eric to have a pet of his own —"

I gave her a grateful smile.

"Of *course*, of course," Mercy said, her voice getting even more sugary. "We *all* want Eric to have his own pet. That would be *so* sweet. It's just . . . *this* pet? I mean, wouldn't he be better off with, say . . . a hamster?"

"Or a goldfish," Faith suggested. "Those smell better than hamsters." Apparently she had forgotten the incident of the little blue fish I'd gotten three years ago. I bet you can guess what happened to him. I'll give you a hint: It was the one time the cats didn't pee on the bed when they got into my room. They were too busy doing something much more evil. Poor Ka-Bluey.

"Yes, something small." Sugar was practically oozing out of Mercy's pores at this point. "So he can learn to take care of it before he moves on to all the responsibility of a dog. Maybe something that would stay in his room all the time, so it won't bother the cats. I mean, they were here first, right? We don't want to *upset* them."

"And they're *so* upset right now," Faith agreed, widening her eyes like she was trying to look pitiful, except it ended up looking more like something was melting inside her head.

"I'm *sure* some other family would *love* to have, er . . . Meatball," Mercy said. "If we take him to the shelter tomorrow, he'll probably have a terrific new home by Saturday. I bet you anything."

"Yeah, Mom," Faith said. "Exactly."

I poked at my baked potato. I didn't feel hungry anymore. I wasn't sure what I thought. I really wanted a dog. And I really didn't want Mercy and Faith to win, like they always did. I definitely did not want another small innocent pet to become an appetizer for Ariadne and Odysseus.

But was Meatball the right dog for me? He was so heavy and . . . snorty. And embarrassing. I mean, when he decided not to walk, there was nothing I could do about it. As if I didn't feel scrawny enough, Meatball would prove it every day. He wasn't anything like perfect Merlin or even funny, smart Buttons. He was kind of a wrinkly, snoring mess. Did I want that kind of chaos in my life? Would it be better to wait and find a less goofy dog?

"Well," Mom said. I could see her starting to give in. She had that resigned look she always gets when Mercy and Faith gang up on her and demand things. "You do make some good points, girls . . ."

"Ahem." At the other end of the table, Tony cleared his throat meaningfully. Mercy and Faith's heads swiveled toward him. They looked surprised, like they'd forgotten he was there. He usually doesn't get involved when they're giving Mom the full-court press.

"Doesn't anyone want to know what Eric thinks?" Tony asked.

Mercy's eyes narrowed. If she'd had claws, I would have warned Tony to protect his eyes.

"Eric?" Faith said, like she had no idea who that was.

"How about it?" Tony said to me. "How do you feel about the big guy so far?"

Mercy laughed in a sort of high-pitched, super-fake way. "Ha-ha-ha! Oh, Eric just thinks a dog is fun. He has no idea how much *work* it's going to be. Really, we just want what's best for him."

"Well, Eric?" Tony said again, ignoring her.

Now they were all staring at me. I had the spooky feeling Odysseus was sitting right below my chair with his claws poised over my defenseless feet, just waiting for me to give the wrong answer.

"Um," I said. "Well . . . I guess . . . I guess I kind of like him."

"Now there's a ringing endorsement," Mercy said, rolling her eyes. "See, Eric's not even that excited. I'm sure he'd *much* prefer a guinea pig."

"No," I said. "Definitely not. No, no, no."

For once, the magic power of three actually worked. "I think we should give it a few more days," Tony said, forking more chicken onto his plate. "If you're right, Mercy, we'll know by next week if Meatball is too much work for Eric. Or maybe he'll grow on all of us. Me, I think he's a great dog. I say let's give him a chance."

"That makes a lot of sense," my mom said, looking pleased. "Good idea, Tony."

Mercy looked about ready to poison all of us. She stabbed her baked potato violently, ignoring Faith's bewildered looks. They'd never lost an argument with Mom before. Faith kept glancing at Mercy like she was waiting for her to jump back in and win it, but Mercy knew she was beaten . . . for now. Neither she nor Faith said another word for the rest of dinner.

It was kind of awesome.

But I knew it wasn't over. Mercy and Faith were on the warpath now. I was definitely not under their radar anymore.

Later that night, I was upstairs working on my pharaoh essay when suddenly there was a quick rapping knock and my bedroom door flew open.

I whirled around and Meatball sat up with a grunt.

"Hi Eric," Mercy said, leaning casually against the doorframe. "What're you doing?"

"Homework," I said. "Why?"

"Oh, I just wanted to see how that dog was fitting in, in here," she said, sliding the door open another inch with her foot. "I mean, it must be such a pain to walk him all the time, when he's so heavy and you're such a shrimp. . . ."

"It's fine," I said. "Careful, don't leave the door —"

But it was too late, and of course that was Mercy's plan. She was holding the door just wide enough for Odysseus to come bolting through. I knew right away that she'd done it on purpose. Mercy had never come into my room before.

The cat darted through the gap and nearly flew onto my bed. I leaped out of my chair and lunged for him, but I wasn't quick enough. He landed on my pillow and stopped to give me an evil, self-satisfied look as he started to squat.

"No!" I yelled.

But someone else got there first. Meatball plowed into the cat's side with his big head, wagging his stumpy tail frantically. He clearly thought Odysseus had jumped up there to play with him. And he was definitely ready to play. He bounced on the bedsprings and batted at Odysseus with his pudgy paws.

His tongue flopped all over the place and he was snorting up a storm.

I don't know if Odysseus had forgotten that Meatball would be there or what. He arched his back and screeched like he was being murdered. In half a second he was flying off the bed again and charging out the door between Mercy's feet.

"Oh my God!" Mercy shrieked. "Did you see that? Faith, come quick! That dog totally attacked Odysseus! Mom!"

Tony came to the door of their bedroom as Mom hurried up from downstairs.

Mercy pointed dramatically at Odysseus's tail, vanishing under the bed in Faith's room. "Look how scared he is! It's all that dog's fault! He's a violent beast!"

"I knew it!" Faith said, jumping up from her desk and running into the hall. "I knew that dog was dangerous! Poor Odysseus! No wonder he's so terrified!"

"Meatball's not dangerous!" I protested. "He was just trying to play, I swear!" Meatball cocked his head to one side so his left ear drooped down. He blinked at me, looking confused, like *What's all the yelling about? Where'd my furry little friend go?*

"See, Mom?" Mercy said triumphantly. "We have to get rid of the dog. He's a menace to the cats."

"Oh, dear," Mom said. "Eric —"

"Wait," Tony said. "Let me get this straight. Meatball was minding his own business in Eric's room. Where Odysseus is not supposed to go — right? So how did the cat even get in there?"

Mom looked at Mercy. My sister folded her arms and shrugged. "I was just asking Eric a question," she said defiantly. "I didn't know the cat was around."

"So it was an accident," Tony said. "And not really Meatball's fault at all." He gave Mercy a look that said *I'm giving you one chance to get out of this.*

Mercy opened and closed her mouth, then scowled at him.

"The point is, that dog could be violent," Faith insisted.

"He doesn't look too violent to me," Tony said, glancing at Meatball's goofy face.

"I don't get that impression either," Mom said. "And Mercy, you know we have to keep the cats out of Eric's room."

Mercy scowled harder and kicked the carpet. "It was an accident," she muttered.

Right. I'm sure.

"That's OK," Tony said. "Just be more careful next time." He leaned into my room to grab the door handle and gave me a wink as he pulled it shut.

I went over to the bed and checked the pillow. Totally dry. It was a miracle.

"Thanks, Meatball," I said, scratching under his chin. "You saved the day."

He panted and grinned at me.

Then I realized he'd left a puddle of drool on my other pillow. So . . . he wasn't quite perfect. But remembering the look on Mercy's face, I decided to forgive him, just this once.

As I fell asleep that night, though, I wondered what I really wanted. I tried to think about the pros and cons of keeping Meatball. I had a lot of time to think about it, because his snoring kept me up for a while. Which really didn't help his case.

Was there a better dog for me out there? A dog that would walk like a normal dog and not slobber all over the girl I liked?

Meatball snorted and rested his head on my foot. On the other hand, I'd never had better protection against the cats. And how sad would he be if I abandoned him too?

What was I going to do?

CHAPTER 10

On the way to school the next morning, Parker suggested that we take all our dogs to the park in the afternoon.

"Yeah! Then Meatball can meet Buttons," Danny said to me. "I just have to get her and Rosie away from Miguel. He usually takes them to the park on Thursdays to lure cheerleaders. It's ridiculous. I'm glad none of us are that dopey about girls . . . *Eric*."

"Shut up," I said. "I'm not dopey."

"Then we can find out if Meatball is also better at playing fetch than Merlin," Parker joked, steering the conversation back to the dogs. Buttons was, like, a master fetcher, which was kind of hilarious because Merlin was so bad at bringing the tennis ball back.

Troy kicked a pile of leaves, frowning. I guessed what he was thinking.

"You'll get a dog soon," I said to him. "Besides, we might not even keep Meatball."

"What?" Parker said. "You have to keep Meatball! He's awesome!"

"I don't know about awesome," I said. "I mean . . . he snores a *lot*. Like, *really loud*." I didn't want to tell them about the bigger problem, which was Meatball's stubbornness. I try not to let the guys know how much my sisters (and their cats) push me around. I didn't want them to know that my dog was doing the same thing.

"Bring him to the park today," Parker said. "Once you see how much fun he is, you'll totally want to keep him."

"Hey, there's Heidi!" Danny said. I looked up and saw a blue bike half a block ahead of us. Heidi's red-blond hair was sticking out from under the bike helmet. "Heidi!" Danny shouted. "Wait up!"

Troy elbowed Parker and nodded at Danny with a grin, but luckily Danny didn't notice. And he said *I* was dopey about girls!

Heidi looked over her shoulder and saw us. She yelled, "Oh, awesome, hey guys!" and tried to wave, and then her bike went one way and she went another, and with a huge *CRASH!* Heidi flew over the handlebars and ended up sprawled across someone's lawn.

We all ran up to her. Danny got there first and helped her to her feet. Her helmet was askew and dirt was scraped across the knees of her jeans. I noticed that she was wearing differently colored socks — one dark blue and one yellow with black polka dots — and I wondered if she'd done that on purpose or by accident. With Heidi it could really be either.

"Oh, man, are you OK?" Parker asked. He went over to pick up her bike.

Heidi started laughing. "Can you believe I did that?" she said. "Jeez, Danny, you should know better than to distract me while I'm biking. Or walking. Or eating. Or doing anything, really. Look at what a disaster I am." She brushed at her jeans and shook her head ruefully when she found a small hole in one knee. "Mom is going to kill me. She just bought me these last week."

"Sorry," Danny said, running one hand through his hair.

"I'll forgive you if you finally let me meet your dog," Heidi said with a grin. She took off her bike helmet and shook out her hair, which was all tangled and messy. Danny took her bike from Parker and started pushing it along beside us as we all walked together.

"How about today?" Danny said. "We're all going to the park after school. You can meet Buttons then, if you want to come." I was impressed at how casually he asked her. If he did like her, he was hiding it well. He acted like he was just one friend talking to another.

"YES!" Heidi nearly shouted. "Seriously? That would be so awesome! Can Ella and Trumpet come?"

Danny looked at us nervously. We hadn't exactly discussed inviting a whole bunch of girls along. Troy and I shrugged.

"Yeah, of course," Parker said. "Eric's dog will be there, too."

"What?" Heidi grabbed my arm and I jumped. "Eric! No way! You have a dog too? What kind?"

"Sort of," I said. "If we keep him. He's a bulldog."

"Isn't that so unfair?" Troy said.

"Aaah, I love bulldogs! What's his name?" Heidi demanded. "I can't believe Cadence was right for once! Maybe she really is psychic."

"Cadence?" I echoed.

"She was telling us yesterday in PE that the vibrations of the universe had told her you'd just gotten a new pet, probably a dog. I was like, no way, I would totally know, all dog news goes through me." Heidi punched Danny's shoulder. "Except apparently when certain of my best friends are involved, *Danny*."

"I said I was sorry about that!" Danny protested. "I didn't think Buttons was a real dog at first!"

"You're a small dog-ist," Heidi said to him. "Small dogs are cute, you dork. And any kind of dog is better than no dog."

"Yeah," Troy said glumly. I wondered if that was true. Would even Heidi want a dog who snored and drooled and refused to walk, like Meatball?

"Cadence isn't psychic," I said. "She saw the dog hair on my jacket on Tuesday."

Heidi laughed. "Silly Cadence," she said, like she thought Cadence was funny instead of crazy and nosy and gossipy.

Danny parked Heidi's bike in the bike racks and she hung her helmet in the bike lock as she locked it up. As we came up the steps into the school, we heard shouting from the sixth-grade hallway. Heidi looked worried and sped up. I recognized the voices of Avery Lafitte and Rory Mason. They were standing in front of our lockers, near Mr. Peary's classroom, yelling at each other. There was a huge crowd of kids standing around watching them fight.

I think I've mentioned Avery before: He's mean all the time, to everyone, for no reason at all. In PE last year, he used to throw any ball he had at me or Troy, acting like it was dodgeball no matter what the game really was. That's until Parker and Danny started doing the same thing to him, and he finally stopped. I'm glad he's in Miss Woodhull's class this year instead of ours.

Rory is our baseball coach's daughter; she's in Mr. Guare's class, and she's good friends with Heidi. They were in the talent show with Ella and her dog, and they actually won with this really funny song.

"She says you took it, Avery!" Rory yelled. Her long brown hair was coming loose from the ponytail she always wears. She usually has a baseball cap on, too, but we're not allowed to wear hats in school.

"I didn't!" Avery yelled back. "She's lying!"

"Cameron wouldn't lie!" Rory shoved him in the chest. She's, like, a foot shorter than Avery, but he still staggered back a step.

"Yeah!" cried a little redheaded girl in the crowd around them. She looked about eight years old. "So there! Meanie!"

"I don't need her stupid lunch money!" Avery shouted. His face was turning red.

"What's going on?" Parker asked Ella, who was standing near the door of our classroom, drumming her fingers nervously on the wall. Nikos Stavros was leaning against the wall beside her with his arms folded.

"Something about Rory's stepsister," Ella said, nodding at the red-haired girl. "I guess she says Avery took her lunch money."

"Jeez, way to be a cliché, Avery," said Nikos. "It's like he has a 'How to Be a Bully' checklist."

"Give it back, Avery!" Danny called. Heidi gave him a weird look, but he didn't see it — I think I was the only one who did.

"Yeah, Avery, stop being a jerk!" Tara Washington yelled.

"How much was it?" Brett Arbus asked, stepping up behind Rory. He pulled out a real wallet from his back pocket and shook back the lock of blond hair that's always falling over his eyes. "I'd be happy to buy this little lady her lunch." He gave Rory and Cameron his charming grin. I didn't think a stunt like that would work on a girl like Rory, but she actually kind of half smiled at him before turning back to Avery.

"It's not about the money," she said. "It's about pushing around a little girl! What kind of freak-show coward are you, Avery?"

Avery clenched his fists. I wondered if he would actually hit Rory. She sure didn't look worried about it. She had her hands on her hips and she was glaring right up at him.

You know what I would never do? Pick a fight with Avery Lafitte. First of all, he's enormous, and second of all, I've heard that he actually takes karate or something. Then again, Rory probably does, too, and nothing seems to scare her.

Danny turned around to say something to Heidi and we realized she wasn't next to us anymore. I saw her pushing through the crowd until she popped out behind Avery. She grabbed Avery's upper arm and he jerked away, but when he saw it was her he stepped back and unclenched his hands.

"Stop fighting!" Heidi said, looking from Avery to Rory. "You guys are both going to get in trouble again!" It's true; the two of them get in trouble all the time — Avery for being mean, and Rory for doing crazy things like skateboarding down the front steps or climbing out a window on the second floor to catch a snail.

Avery kicked the nearest locker so hard I thought he must have broken his toe. "I didn't steal any stupid lunch money," he said to Heidi.

"Cameron says he did!" Rory snapped. "Why would she lie about that?"

"Maybe there's a mistake," Heidi said, looking

flustered. She crouched down to talk to Rory's stepsister. "Hey, Cameron, did you maybe just lose it?"

"No!" Cameron said, twirling a lock of red hair around one finger. "It was in my backpack and then it was gone! He took it!" She pointed dramatically at Avery, who made a horrible scowly face at her.

"Out of your backpack?" Rory said. "I thought you said he took it from you."

"He did!" Cameron protested. "It was mine!"

"But did you see him take it out of your backpack?" Heidi asked.

Cameron stamped her foot and scrunched up her face like she was about to cry. "I know he did! I know he took it! He's mean!"

Rory ran her hand over the top of her head like she wasn't sure what to do.

"What is all this?" a new voice boomed. Vice Principal Taney was charging down the hall toward us from his office. His long sharp nose was like an arrow aimed straight at Rory and Avery, and his white eyebrows were frowning so hard it looked like they might just crawl right off his face.

Everybody scattered into their classrooms as fast as they could. Mr. Taney is a scary man. Only Rory, Heidi, Avery, and Cameron stayed where they were.

They couldn't exactly escape — Mr. Taney was pointing right at them.

Parker and Danny and I hurried into Mr. Peary's classroom, crashing into Ella and Nikos and Rebekah in the doorway. I hadn't even seen Rebekah arrive with all the commotion. She was wearing a green T-shirt with a gray cat on it.

"Sir, it's just a misunderstanding —" Heidi was saying in the hall behind us.

"Detention, all of you!" I heard Mr. Taney yell.

"Poor Heidi," I said. "She was just trying to help." I thought I was talking to Danny, but when I turned around, he was already halfway across the room, and it was just Rebekah right next to me.

"Seriously!" Rebekah said. "But it's not like Eyebrows out there is going to care who actually did what."

I didn't know what to say, so I just shrugged as we sat down at our desks. Mr. Peary hurried in with a stack of books. There was just one minute until the bell rang; usually he's there way before us.

"Of course he did it," I heard Brett say to Jonas and Nikos. "It's totally the kind of thing Avery would do."

"Innocent until proven guilty," Nikos said with a shrug.

"Not in sixth grade," Brett said. "Try telling Taney that."

"Oh, Eric," Rebekah said. "I brought you something." She picked up her purple book bag and started digging through it.

I stared at her. Something for me?

"Here." She handed me a paperback — *The Book of Three*, by Lloyd Alexander. It had a guy in a cloak riding a horse on the cover. "It's one of my favorites."

"Oh," I said, turning it over in my hands. "Uh — I — um —"

"You don't have to read it," she said quickly. "Only if you want to. I'm afraid it doesn't have a bulldog in it, but it *does* have a pig that can see the future, which is kind of the same, right?"

I could hardly keep up with this conversation. "A pig that can see the future?"

"You'll like it," she said, and just then the bell rang.

"Um, OK," I said. "Thanks."

Mr. Peary started talking, but I couldn't concentrate. I was thinking that I should ask Rebekah to come to the park with us, the way Danny had invited Heidi. She could bring Noodles. It would be kind of like asking her out, wouldn't it? But then I could pretend like that's not what I meant if she laughed in my face. I just had to sound all casual and "whatever" like Danny did.

I thought about asking her all morning. Finally I decided to ask her at lunch; sometimes she sat with me and the guys if Heidi and Kristal and Ella were sitting with us. But on the way to the cafeteria, Heidi told us she had to spend lunch in the principal's office.

"Sorry, guys," she said, looking really upset. "I have to stay for detention after school, so I can't come to the park with you."

"Is your mom going to be mad?" Danny asked.

"Oh, yes," Heidi said. I tried to remember if I'd ever seen Heidi not smiling before. She looked like missing out on our dogs was the saddest thing that had ever happened to her.

"Don't worry," Danny said. "We'll go to the park tomorrow, or this weekend, or sometime soon."

"If my mom lets me!" Heidi said. "Mr. Taney said we'd have detention for at least a week."

"That's so unfair," Ella said warmly, giving Heidi a one-armed hug. "You didn't do anything wrong!"

"Stupid Avery," Danny said. He sounded really mad.

"It's not his fault," Heidi said. "I think Cameron really did just lose her lunch money. She couldn't explain why she thought he took it. She just kept saying 'He's so mean! I know he did!' over and over."

"Well, he *is* mean," Ella pointed out.

Heidi laughed. "Still," she said.

"Don't worry," Danny said again. "Buttons isn't going anywhere."

"Same with Merlin," Parker said.

They all looked at me. "Uh, yeah. And Meatball," I said, although I wasn't sure it was true.

Now I couldn't ask Rebekah to join us. It would be too weird if she came and no other girls did. Plus I'd never hear the end of it from the guys. And she didn't sit with us at lunch anyway. Without Heidi around, Ella went to the music room and Kristal and Rebekah sat with their other friends.

I knew I wouldn't have been able to do it even if everything had turned out right. Every time I thought about how the question would sound, my mouth got dry and my stomach started flapping around like Meatball's face.

But it was actually a good thing I didn't ask her, because as it turned out, Meatball at the park was a complete disaster.

CHAPTER 11

First of all, it took us practically an hour just to *get* to the park. Meatball really, really wanted to sniff *everything* that he passed. If I tried to drag him forward, he planted his butt on the sidewalk and refused to move until I let him sniff his brains out. I kept saying, "Meatball, we're going to the park! It'll be more fun there, I swear! The guys are waiting for us! Come *on*!" But that didn't make any difference. He would not be hurried.

So Parker and Danny and Troy had been waiting for ages by the time we got there. I could hear them calling Merlin and Buttons as we came up to the gate into the dog run. Meatball heard it, too; his ears flipped forward and he even sped up a little bit.

We went through the double gates and I unhooked his leash. He stood there for a moment, sniffing the gravel and casting suspicious looks sideways at the other two dogs, who were running around the other end of the dog run.

“Hiiiiiiiiiiiiiiiiiiiiiiiiiiiiiiiiiii Eric!” Rosie called, jumping up on a bench and waving at me.

“It’s about time!” Danny shouted.

Merlin and Buttons spotted Meatball and came charging over. Meatball kind of jumped back a step and braced his shoulders, watching them warily with his big brown eyes. Buttons started bouncing around his paws, trying to jump up and sniff his face. Merlin politely circled him for a minute, wagging his silky golden tail like he was saying *Hey friend, nothing to worry about, chill out.*

“Whoa,” Danny said, jogging up to us with the others close behind him. “That is one fat dog.”

“Danny, don’t be rude,” Rosie said bossily. She had her curly dark hair parted in two braids with little glittery pink clips at the ends and she was wearing a pink T-shirt that said: PRINCESSES RULE. On the back it said: LITERALLY. “That’s how bulldogs are supposed to look,” she added. “Right, Eric?”

“As far as I know,” I said.

“He’s no bloodhound,” Troy said to me, giving Meatball his detective face. “But he’s cool. Check out how flat his nose is. How does he even breathe?”

“Loudly,” I said. Meatball was demonstrating his *chug-a-chug-a SNARR SNARR* breathing noises right that second. Buttons kept jumping back like she thought he was growling at her, but that was just how he sounded when he inhaled.

"Hey Meatball," Parker said, crouching and letting Meatball sniff his hand. Merlin immediately came over and tried to stuff his head under Parker's arm.

Rosie put her hands on her hips and studied Meatball from tip to tail. His brow was all furrowed and he kept twitching away from the other two dogs when they tried to sniff his butt. His eyes rolled sideways as he tried to watch them both at once.

"Hmm," Rosie said. "He's not a very *you* kind of dog, Eric."

"What does that mean?" Parker asked.

"He's, like — drooling and stuff," Rosie said. "And he's so — loud." Meatball gave a long snort, as if to prove her point. "Eric isn't loud," Rosie pointed out.

"He does drool, though," Danny joked.

"Shut up," I said, punching his shoulder. I didn't say anything out loud, but I kind of agreed with Rosie. That was exactly what I'd been worrying about all week. Meatball didn't seem like my kind of dog at all.

"This dog is more like *you* than Eric," Rosie said to Danny. "But no, you can't have one," she added quickly.

"I'll take him if you don't want him," Troy said to me.

"Right. Your mom would be psyched about that," Parker said, and Troy sighed. I like Troy's mom, but she worries about a lot of things, so I'm guessing she wouldn't be thrilled about all the drooling and snoring.

Merlin got bored of trying to make friends with Meatball and trotted off to find the tennis ball. Buttons swiveled her fluffy little head back and forth between them, trying to decide whether the curiously wrinkled new guy was more interesting than her sleek, shiny best friend. Finally, she sprang to her paws and chased after Merlin.

Meatball sat down with what sounded like a relieved sigh.

"What's the matter with you?" I said to him. "Don't you want to play with them? You had no problem playing with —" I stopped myself just in time. Telling the guys about Rebekah and Noodles was the last thing I wanted to do.

"Playing with who?" Rosie asked.

"Er . . . my sister's cats," I said lamely.

"Really?" Parker said, raising his eyebrows in a surprised way. "But your cats hate everyone."

"Oh, they hate him, too," I said. "It's kind of one-sided playing."

"Maybe he just needs to warm up," Parker said, digging a tennis ball out of his pocket. "Here, throw this for him."

I knelt down and let Meatball sniff the tennis ball all over. His eyes nearly crossed as he peered at the ball at the end of his flat snout. His squashed-up nose scrunched up and down as he inhaled its scent. He opened his mouth and smooshed his jowls around the ball, chewing it between his teeth.

I wrestled it away from him and said, "OK, Meatball! Fetch!" And then I flung the tennis ball as far as I could down the dog run.

Meatball didn't even stand up. He just tipped back his head and gazed at me with his puzzled expression, like *Well, that was weird. Where'd it go?*

"Go on!" I said, pointing after the ball. "Go get it!"

Meatball stared blankly in the direction I was pointing, and then looked up at me again. He blinked a couple of times and then yawned hugely.

Buttons came galloping over with the tennis ball wedged in her tiny mouth. She dropped it at my feet and made a play bow, wagging her tail.

Rosie clapped her hands. "That's my little genius!" she said happily.

Danny grabbed the ball and threw it, and Buttons went racing after it.

"See?" I said to Meatball. "Like that."

He stood up, shook himself (*flap flap flap* went his face), and came over to lean against my leg.

Parker laughed. "I guess he's not the fetching type."

"He's as bad as a cat," I said disgustedly. At least Merlin would *chase* the ball, even if he wasn't great at bringing it back.

And it didn't get any better the rest of the time we were there. Merlin and Buttons ran and played and jumped in the water fountain and barked and chased each other in circles. They were having the best time ever. Meatball, on the other hand, fell asleep on my feet the minute I sat down on the bench. And, of course, he snored. And drooled on my sneakers.

I was really glad Rebekah wasn't there to see it.

"This is going on the 'con' side of the list," I said to him, leaning my elbows on my knees. "'Doesn't know how to play.' That's kind of a bad sign for a dog, man."

Troy sat down on the bench next to me. "Talking to yourself?" he said. He took off his baseball cap and tried to smooth down his red hair.

"To this lumpy lump of fur," I said, nudging Meatball's chin with the sneaker he was drooling on.

"Maybe he just plays differently than the other two," Troy said. "Like Nikos doesn't play baseball, but he's a whiz at video games."

"Yeah, sure," I said. "I just need to get Meatball a doggy Nintendo."

"Bulldog Kong," Troy suggested. "Super Meatball Kart."

"Drool Kombat," I said, and he laughed.

But I worried about it all the way home. Especially when Meatball noticed how close we were to Rebekah's house and tried to haul me over there, and we had this way embarrassing tug-of-war right there on the sidewalk, which I only won by wrapping my arms around a tree and holding my ground until he got bored.

Was Meatball more trouble than he was worth? If he couldn't even run around the dog run with me . . . was that the kind of dog I wanted?

"Hey Eric!" Tony called from the living room when he heard us come in the back door. "You're missing the game!"

I hung Meatball's leash on the door and left him with his face buried in his food bowl. Tony was in his easy chair watching the baseball game. I gotta say, this is the number one best thing about having a stepdad. I never, ever got to watch any sports when I was living with just Mom and Mercy and Faith, except maybe women's basketball and, like, Olympic ice-skating. Seriously. I know way more about Kimmie Meisner and Sasha Cohen than any eleven-year-old guy is supposed to know.

I wanted to sit down and join him, but Ariadne was lying across the top of the couch, and she started lashing her long gray tail angrily the minute I walked in.

"It's only the second inning," Tony said with his eyes on the screen. "Your mom said we could order Chinese tonight."

"Great," I said, eyeing the cat. "I'll, uh — just go put my stuff down."

"Wait till the next commercial break," Tony said, waving at the couch. "This is a good game."

I carefully sat down, pressed into the corner as far away from Ariadne as I could get. She glowered at me for a minute, then got up and stretched slowly, extending her needle-sharp claws way out in front of her. She jumped down to the couch cushion and started pacing toward me with slow, deliberate steps, like she was stalking me but didn't care that I could see her coming.

I kind of wanted to get up and run out of the room, but I thought that would look really lame in front of Tony. Instead I took the side cushion and stuck it between me and Ariadne. She gave me a look like *Really? You think that'll stop me?* and sat down just within clawing distance of me. Her yellow eyes stared and stared at me. It was pretty hard to focus on the game that way.

"Meatball!" I called, and winced at the way my voice wobbled.

From the kitchen, the only response was *crunch crunch crunch snorft snorft crunch snooorrrrrft.* So much for my fearless bodyguard.

"Yes!" Tony shouted at the screen. "Run! Go! Home run! Come on!"

I leaned forward, watching the ball fly into the outfield, and while we were both distracted, Ariadne struck. She leaped onto the cushion and lashed out at me.

"Ow!" I yelped, jumping to my feet. A long thin

scratch ran down my arm, already welling tiny spots of blood. Ariadne flew up the stairs and almost immediately I heard my sisters' feet come running.

"What did you do to Ariadne?" Mercy yelled from the top of the stairs.

"What did *I* do?!"

Meatball came galloping in from the kitchen, all *What'd I miss? What'd I miss?* Dopey useless furball.

"Let me see," Tony said, taking my arm. "Yikes. She really got you."

"It's OK. I'm used to it," I said. "It's my fault for sitting so close to her."

My stepdad gave me a look like I was brain-dead. "You're allowed to sit on your own couch," he said.

Meatball had already come to that conclusion. He sprawled happily across the cushions with his tongue flapping as he panted.

"It's no big deal," I said, sitting down next to Meatball.

"I'm getting the first aid kit," Tony said, pressing his lips together. I said he didn't have to, but he was already halfway to the kitchen.

"Whiner," Mercy said from the bottom of the stairs, glancing down the hall to make sure Tony couldn't hear her.

"I said it's no big deal," I said.

“Aww, poor tiny Eric, scared of a fluffy little cat,” Faith said. She leaned over the stair rail and handed something to Mercy.

“What —” I started to say, and then blinked as a flash went off in my face. When I could see again, Mercy was handing the camera back to Faith.

“Why’d you do that?” I asked.

“No reason,” she said with a sweet smile. Then my sisters both vanished up the stairs as quickly as Ariadne, escaping before Tony came back with Band-Aids and antibiotic ointment.

Meatball snored on, unconcerned, with a corner of his tongue sticking out under his nose. But I knew enough to be worried. What had they taken a picture of? What were they planning to do with it?

Whatever it was, knowing Mercy and Faith . . . I wasn’t going to like it.

CHAPTER 12

I found out what they were up to the very next day.

On Fridays we had computer lab for an hour after lunch, which was my favorite part of the week. Usually there was an assignment like "find the answers to these ten questions on the Internet" or "make a pie chart using this data and Microsoft Excel," but it was always really easy. And when I finished, Mr. Peary let me work on other things, like the website I was trying to build about Harry Houdini. The problem was finding a way to make the site interesting that hadn't been done by all the other Houdini websites.

I was working on the header graphic, trying to make it appear and disappear, when I heard a little gasp from Rebekah's computer, three seats away. I glanced over at her, but she was frowning at her screen. Then suddenly she looked straight at me . . . and frowned even more!

"What?" I whispered. Brett was on the computer next to me and he looked over with a confused expression like he thought I was talking to him.

"I can't believe you!" Rebekah whispered back.

Uh-oh. She sounded really mad. "What?" I said again. "Why?" I knew right away my sisters must have done something. I remembered the photo and thought about all the terrible things they might have done with it. Had they posted me on, like, a dating site or something? But then how would Rebekah have found it? Our computers had all these blocks on them so we couldn't get to those sites.

"You know what!" Rebekah said. "That poor dog! Do you know how sad they are in shelters?" In between us, Heidi and Brett looked back and forth like they were at a tennis match. Heidi's ears had practically perked up when Rebekah said "dog."

I checked over my shoulder and saw that Mr. Peary was sitting next to Jonas, explaining something on the keyboard. He had his back to us. I got up and tiptoed over to Rebekah's computer.

Unfortunately, Tara and Natasha were sitting across from Rebekah. They saw me crouch down beside her and they started giggling.

Rebekah ignored them and pointed to her screen. My first thought was that the photo was really bad. I was making this doofy face that made me look as dopey as Meatball. Most of the photo was of him. His fat white paws drooped off the side of the couch and his face was smushed up by the cushions under him.

It took me a minute to figure out what I was looking at. At the top of the screen was a headline that said: *Bulldog needs a new home!*

Then I realized. It was an ad on the school bulletin board!

My sisters had posted Meatball's photo online, trying to get someone to take him away. I read the whole ad, getting madder and madder. They'd written it pretending to be me! It was all about how hard it was to take care of such a big dog, and how I really wanted to find a good home for him, but if I didn't he was going to a shelter on Sunday, so it was an emergency. It made me sound like kind of a jerk who didn't care about my dog at all. Plus there were a ton of misspelled words that spell-check would definitely have caught. As if I would post something with that many mistakes on the Internet!

"I didn't post this," I said to Rebekah. I was so

mad, I forgot to be nervous around her. "I don't want to get rid of Meatball." *At least . . . I don't think I do. Definitely not like this, anyway!* "My sisters must have done it."

"But why?" Rebekah said. "That's so mean!"

"They don't like Meatball," I said. "Or me, for that matter."

"What's going on?" Heidi asked, leaning over to peek at Rebekah's screen. "Is that a picture of your dog?"

"Nothing," I said, covering it with my hands. "Just my sisters being obnoxious."

"Oooooooooooooo," Tara said, loud enough for everyone to hear. "Rebekah and Eric have *secrets*, ooooooooooooooo." Natasha started giggling again and glanced over at Parker.

"Eric, please return to your own computer," Mr. Peary said. "And Tara, no talking."

I hurried back to my seat, my face on fire. I was embarrassed, but I was also mad. Mercy and Faith had no right to do that! Poor Meatball! What would they do next? Give him away while no one else was home?

Not on my watch. This time their evil plans would not succeed.

An e-mail from Rebekah popped up with the ad attached. The message said: *Don't let them get away with it!*

I won't, I wrote back.

I printed the ad and took it home with me. I didn't say anything to Mercy and Faith when they got home. I stayed in my room, because I thought I might yell at them if I saw them, and I wanted to wait until I had backup.

At dinner they were both smiling like Queen Yesinda, this evil character who always turns up right when I'm about to lose my favorite computer game. Mom didn't notice, but Tony kept giving them thoughtful looks like he was wondering what they were up to.

I waited until we were all sitting down with our tuna and broccoli casserole. I waited until both Mercy and Faith had their mouths full. And then I whipped the ad out of my back pocket, unfolded it, and slapped it on the table in front of Mom.

Mercy's eyebrows went up when she saw what it was.

"Mom," I said, and I was proud to hear that my voice wasn't even shaking very much. "Look what Mercy and Faith did."

Faith rolled her eyes and sighed like I was *so* immature.

Mom scanned the page, her forehead crinkling kind of like Meatball's. "What is this?" she asked. "Eric, does this mean you don't want Meatball after all?"

"No!" I said. "No, no, no. That's the point. Mercy and Faith wrote this and posted it online. They were trying to get rid of him! Without asking the rest of us!"

"Let me see that," Tony said, holding out his hand. I passed the printout to him and he frowned as he read it.

"Tattletale," Mercy said to me.

"Brat," Faith added.

"Yeah, well, you guys are jerks," I said.

"That's enough name-calling," Mom said. "Girls, why did you do this?"

"We were trying to *help*," Mercy said, switching instantly into her fake-sweet voice. "We thought if we found a nice *home* for Meatball, then Eric would feel better about giving him up. Since we know he really *wants* to, he just feels badly about it."

"Who knows why?" Faith interjected. "It's not like that dog cares if we don't keep him."

"Meatball would care!" I said. "He'd care a lot more than your cats, who don't like anybody, not even you!"

Mercy and Faith both looked outraged — and really shocked that I'd said anything back to them. "Ariadne and Odysseus were here first!" Mercy snapped. "This is their home!"

"It's mine, too!" I said. "I can't do anything without those cats coming after me! I want —" I took a deep breath. "I want to keep Meatball." There. I'd said it. There was no going back now.

I noticed Tony hide a grin behind his napkin.

"No!" Faith said. "We already found someone to take him!"

Mom drew in her breath sharply, and Mercy finally looked a little nervous, like she knew they'd gone too far.

"First of all," Mom said, "what is our rule about contacting strangers over the Internet?"

Faith looked down at her plate and kicked the table leg.

"I hope you haven't given this person our address," Mom said sternly.

"We haven't written back yet," Mercy said, frowning sullenly. "But I'm sure it's fine. The guy said he was always looking for tough dogs."

“Meatball isn’t tough,” I said. I could only imagine what this guy needed “tough” dogs for. “He’s lazy and friendly. And I’m keeping him.”

“We should get some say, too!” Mercy whined. “Mooom! We don’t *want* a big smelly dog! Why does Eric get to decide? There’s *two* of us, and *we* don’t want him!”

“Yeah!” Faith agreed.

“Well,” Tony spoke up at last. “Personally, I like Meatball. Which I guess makes two of us who *do* want him.”

Mercy and Faith gaped at him. I looked at Mom. She stuck her fork into a piece of broccoli and pushed it around her plate for a second. Then she looked up and smiled at me and Tony.

“Actually,” she said, “that makes three of us.”

CHAPTER 13

Hoo boy. You have never seen anyone madder than Mercy and Faith right then. The funny thing is, if they hadn't posted the ad — if they had waited a few days like Tony suggested — maybe we would have decided not to keep Meatball after all. It was seeing how awful Mercy and Faith could be that made up my mind. That and picturing poor loyal Meatball all alone in a shelter, waiting patiently for me to come rescue him.

On the other hand, I think we might have decided to keep him anyway. I guess, despite the snoring, he was kind of growing on me. So all that really happened was that Mercy and Faith got in big trouble for posting the ad. They were grounded for two weeks, which meant they couldn't go anywhere after school except basketball practice. There was a lot of yelling about plans they'd made — I heard them shouting about George a few times — but Mom was firm.

When I got back upstairs, Meatball was waiting right inside the door to my room, like he somehow knew what had happened downstairs. His eyes were wrinkled up in his smiley way and his butt was wagging hard enough to nearly knock him over.

I crouched and gave him a hug around his broad shoulders. He slurped his tongue up my cheek.

"I guess we're stuck with each other now," I said, scratching behind his ears.

I got up to go to my computer and stopped, thinking. Instead of closing my door, I opened it wider, so Meatball and I could see the hall and the stairs. Meatball immediately lay down across the doorway with his nose sticking out into the hall, like he was guarding the room. He sighed happily, making the beige carpet fibers flutter.

"Good boy," I said with a grin. *Let's see Ariadne and Odysseus try to get in here now!* Later I noticed that Mercy and Faith both had *their* doors shut for once. I hoped they were just sulking instead of plotting something new. But after the scene at dinner, I had a feeling they'd be licking their wounds for a while.

Tony stopped on his way to bed and gave Meatball a belly rub.

"Thanks," I said, spinning my chair around. "That was cool, what you did."

"You started it," Tony said with a grin. "You were cool first. Sticking up for Meatball like that."

"Well," I said, "I figure he would have done the same for me."

Tony laughed. "Yeah, that's true," he said. "Bulldogs are famously loyal. And I think he's attached himself to you pretty well."

"I hope it works out," I said. "He's not what I expected a dog to be like."

"No dog is," Tony said. "You'd be surprised. Apart from my Lab, I had a few German shepherds while I was growing up, and they were all different in funny ways. As dogs go, I get the feeling Meatball is one of the good ones."

"Snarrgarrgarrrggah," Meatball agreed, wriggling on his back and batting Tony with one stiff paw.

"He's a lot braver than me," I said. "Maybe I should try to be more like him."

Tony made a face. "Not in the drooling sense, I hope."

I grinned. "I'm sorry Mercy and Faith are going to be so mad at you."

He shrugged. "Don't worry. I've got a line on some WNBA tickets that I think will help smooth things over."

"Wow, yeah," I said. "That'll definitely help."

After he left, I signed in to chat. I felt like a different person. Someone who was brave like Harry Houdini. Someone who said exactly what he thought and fought for what was right and didn't let a couple of cats — or a couple of sisters — push him around.

I thought about how Meatball just charged into things with no fear. Like couches with cats on them or other people's yards. He just lowered his head and braced his shoulders and went for it. He was too excited and optimistic to worry about what would happen.

I was lucky. During that brief spurt of courage, "Maltizu" was signed on.

Hey Rebekah, I wrote. **What R U doing tomorrow?**

CHAPTER 14

Of course, by the time I got up on Saturday morning, I was a nervous wreck again. What kind of crazy person had taken over my fingers and asked Rebekah to go to the park with me and Meatball? Did I really want her to see him at his most boring? Poor Noodles would probably end up in a boredom coma when she saw how lame Meatball could be.

But I couldn't get out of it now. I'd told her I would bring Meatball over at eleven o'clock. Then I'd stayed up half the night reading the book she gave me. Mostly I read nonfiction, like biographies and stuff, but *The Power of Three* was actually really good. It was funnier than I thought it would be. I didn't have time to finish it, but I figured at least I could tell her that I started it.

Mom was reorganizing the pantry when Meatball and I came down to the kitchen. Once a month she has these organizing fits and pulls everything out of a cupboard, scatters it all over the floor, and then gets distracted halfway through and shoves everything back in again. I could tell she was already getting to that stage by the way she was mashing cereal boxes in next to the rice and pasta without even alphabetizing them or anything.

"I'm taking Meatball to the park," I said, lifting his leash from the door handle.

"Call me if you're not coming home for lunch," she said, her voice muffled by the stacks of cans around her head. "You can take my cell phone; it's on the table. I'll just be here."

"Thanks," I said, putting the phone in my pocket. I was pretty sure I would be home for lunch. I had a feeling I'd be home in ten minutes, when either (a) Rebekah got fed up and went home, or (b) I chickened out and ditched her.

But there was no way Meatball was letting me wriggle out of this. He didn't even stop to sniff anything as he barreled along the path to her house. His paws drove into the sidewalk and he leaned forward with this furrowed, determined expression like he was dragging an entire eighteen-wheeler truck behind him instead of just skinny old me. I swear the soles of my sneakers must have been nearly burned off by me trying to slow him down. It was like water-skiing or dogsledding on the sidewalk, only I didn't have a sled or skis.

Rebekah and Noodles were on the porch playing with a squeaky toy shaped like a panda. Rebekah waved as we screeched up to the fence, and Meatball slammed his face into the posts, snorting ecstatically.

"Come inside," Rebekah called as we came through the gate. "I'm sorry I'm not ready yet, but I was going to do everything this morning and then Heidi called and was totally freaking out about something and I'm not even sure what it was but I don't think I helped."

"Inside?" I said, trying to get to the point of her sentence. What was the "everything" she was going to do? What was wrong with Heidi? "With Meatball? Are you sure?"

"Yeah, why not?" she said. "He's a good dog. Aren't you, Meatball?"

Meatball went *SNOOOOOOOOOOORT,* which for some reason Rebekah decided was a yes. We followed her inside the house and she unclipped Meatball's leash before I could warn her not to. He bolted off into the living room and I heard a thud, which I guessed was him leaping onto the couch.

"EEEEEEEEE!!!" went someone in the living room.

“Uh-oh.” I ran after Meatball with Noodles at my feet yipping excitedly.

Meatball was, in fact, up on the big blue couch in the living room. He had a small brown-haired girl pinned under his meaty paws and he was licking her face and her arms as she tried to ward him off, shrieking.

“I’m sorry!” I cried. “Meatball! Bad! Meatball, leave her alone!” I ran over and grabbed his collar, but he was too heavy and determined, and in the end I had to wrap my whole body around him to wrestle him away from her.

He flopped back against the opposite arm of the couch and went *hhaaahhhhaaaahhh snrrrrrrsnrrrrsnrrrr* with an enormous grin.

“I’m so, so, *so* sorry,” I said, keeping my arms outstretched so he wouldn’t lunge past me again. The little girl was making funny hiccupping noises and I felt a bolt of terror that Meatball had made her cry or set off an asthma attack or something terrible.

But finally I realized she was laughing.

“Your dog is crazy!” she giggled, wiping her face with her sleeves. “You’re a crazy dog!” she said to Meatball.

“Eric, this is my sister, Elisabeth,” Rebekah said, perching in a chair nearby. “We call her Ellie.”

"Uh — hi," I said.

"I'm eight. I'm in third grade," Ellie said. "I can write in cursive! And add up big numbers! I'm really good at it!"

"Oh — uh — awesome," I said. Meatball rested his chin on my shoulder and slobbered a little. Then he sat up and went "RRFF! Rrrrrfff!"

Ellie giggled again. "He sounds so serious next to Noodles!"

"Yeah, his voice is much deeper," Rebekah said.

"RROOOOFF," Meatball insisted.

"He hardly ever barks," I said. "I have no idea what this is about."

"I do," Rebekah said, nodding at the back of the couch behind me. "He's saying hi to Carbonel."

I twisted around and nearly had a heart attack. A cat was sitting on top of the cushion right behind me, and he looked *exactly* like Odysseus. He had the same thick black fur and intense yellow eyes and feathery ears. For a moment I actually thought maybe Odysseus had followed me to Rebekah's like an evil shadow.

I don't know if Rebekah saw the expression of terror that must have shot across my face, but she said, "Don't worry, he's friendly."

Carbonel stretched elegantly, one paw at a time,

and then he stepped delicately along the cushion until he was standing over Meatball. The bulldog squirmed around and stuck his squashy face up until he was flat black nose to little pink nose with the cat. Both of their noses twitched as they went *sniff sniff sniff sniff sniff sniff.*

"Uh . . . his name is Carbonel?" I said to Rebekah.

Her face lit up. "Don't you know the Carbonel books? He's the King of Cats! I'll lend you those next."

"I read all the time," Ellie announced. "See, those are my library books, and those are Rebekah's." She pointed to two piles of books on the side table. "The library is my favorite place in the whole wide world."

I jumped as Carbonel made a sudden movement beside me. He had dropped to his stomach and was batting at Meatball's nose with his front paws. But his claws were sheathed, and he was purring. I have never, ever heard Ariadne or Odysseus purr. I guess if they ever do, they stop when I get close enough to hear it.

Meatball pulled his head back, wrinkling his forehead at the cat for a second. Then he stood up on his back legs and propped his front paws on the top of the couch on either side of Carbonel. The black cat rolled onto his back and batted at Meatball's loose jowls hanging down over him.

"Hhrruuff!" Meatball woofed, nosing the cat's stomach.

Noodles decided that was quite enough attention she wasn't getting, and she went "ARRUFF! Ruff! Ruff!" from the floor.

Rebekah laughed. "OK, wait here," she said to me. "I'll be back in a minute." She ran off to the kitchen as Meatball rolled heavily off the couch and snort-poked at Noodles.

Left alone, Carbonel sat up and licked his paws for a moment, like *Oh, fine, I was done playing anyway.* I tried not to be too obvious about watching him, but I couldn't help feeling like I was about to get clawed.

"Are you Rebekah's boyfriend?" Ellie asked out of the blue.

"Uh — I — no — I mean — no — uh —" I must have stammered about twenty meaningless syllables before Carbonel decided to put me out of my misery and leaped down into my lap. I froze, but he just turned in a circle, poked my knee with his paw, and then lay down in a little ball of black fur.

"Are you afraid of cats?" Ellie asked. "That's funny if you are. I like cats."

"I like cats," I said, not very convincingly. Of course, the cats I like don't usually look exactly like my arch-nemesis. I gingerly patted Carbonel's back. His ears twitched, and I felt a rumble go through his fur. He was purring!

"You have a very purry cat," I said to Ellie.

"I know," she said. "He loves everyone."

"My sisters' cats don't like anyone," I said.

Rebekah's dad poked his head in the door. "Hey there. You must be Eric."

I didn't know whether to stand up and displace Carbonel to shake his hand, or if it would be rude to just keep sitting there. But Mr. Waters waved me down before I could move. "Stay where you are. I'm covered in paint anyway. Tell Rebekah to stop by the garage before you head off to the park, OK?"

"OK," Ellie and I said at the same time. He waved again and we heard him clomp out the side door.

Rebekah came hurrying back in carrying a bulging plastic bag.

"What's that?" Ellie said curiously.

"Eric and I are going for a picnic in the park," Rebekah said.

We are? I thought.

"I made sandwiches," she hurried on. "You like

peanut butter, right, Eric? I've seen you bring it for lunch sometimes."

"Uh, sure," I said. "Yeah. Awesome."

"Good," Rebekah said. "Because it's the only lunch I know how to make!"

"Dad said to go to the garage before you go," Ellie announced.

"OK. Ready, Eric?" Rebekah scooped up Noodles with her free arm and hung her over one shoulder while she grabbed her leash. Noodles was kind of like a fluffy scarf; she was easy to pick up, she stayed wherever you put her, and even if she tried to plant her butt and stay in one place, there was no way she would win.

Boy, would my life be different with a dog like that. But then, I bet the cats would totally push around a little dog. I'd feel bad if Ariadne and Odysseus were picking on a dog like Noodles. At least Meatball could take care of himself.

"'Bye, Ellie," I said, clipping Meatball's leash on again. She waved, though her nose was already back in her book. I followed Rebekah out the side door into her driveway. There was a garage set far back at the end, separate from the house. It was surrounded by piles of boxes and mountains of stuff. From inside the garage, I could hear hammering and sawing.

"Mom and Dad are putting up new shelves. They're trying to get the garage cleaned up so we can actually maybe put the car in it this winter," Rebekah explained.

"Rebekah," her mom called from the garage doorway. "Would you just check that box and make sure you don't want to keep anything in there?" She pointed at a big cardboard box over on the side, next to an old tricycle and a pink skateboard with glittery lightning stickers on it.

"Sure," Rebekah answered, and her mom waved at me before disappearing into the garage again. Meatball and I followed Rebekah over to the box. Rebekah handed me Noodles's leash and started digging through the stuff inside.

Noodles pawed at my leg and tipped her head up so her fluffy ears flipped back as she looked up at me. I crouched down and patted her while Meatball nosed around the box, wheezing. Her fur was really soft, like what you'd think clouds might feel like. She wrapped her front paws around my hand so I could scratch under her chin. Her little tail was swishing back and forth and her soft brown eyes were perfectly round. She couldn't be more different from Meatball, but the funny thing was, they both had these cute, goofy, openmouthed smiles.

Something went *CLATTER CLATTER* around the side of the box.

"Meatball, leave it, whatever it is," I said, tugging on the end of his leash. Of course that didn't budge him even a little. I could see his butt sticking out, and it was wriggling, so I knew he was excited about something.

"It's all right," Rebekah said. "There's nothing he can break over here. Mom! Are you kidding? You can't throw out my *Guardians of Ga'Hoole* books! I love these books!" She started digging paperbacks out of the box.

"I thought you'd read them all!" her mom called back.

"So?" Rebekah said. "What if I want to read them again? Or lend them to my friends?"

Meatball's butt vanished behind the box. I picked up Noodles and went to see what he was doing.

My mouth fell open.

Meatball was skateboarding!

CHAPTER 15

Well, he was sort of skateboarding. He had the pink skateboard flipped onto its wheels and was nudging it back and forth with his nose. As I watched, he put one paw on the board and walked along beside it for a minute. Then he put both his front paws on it and stood there, thinking. His brow was furrowed like he was concentrating really hard on figuring this out. His tongue was going *flap flap flap* like a sail again as he panted and thought and wobbled around on the skateboard.

Finally he got it moving by pushing with his back paws while his front paws were on it. Then he scrambled to get all his paws on at once, and the skateboard slowed to a stop. Undaunted, Meatball put one fat paw down and pushed — and he was rolling! I dropped his leash and let him go.

"Arrgaarraarrrgah!" Meatball gargle-barked triumphantly. He put his two left paws down and pushed again. The skateboard went flying across the driveway with him on top.

"Oh my gosh!" Rebekah shrieked. "Look! Mom, Dad, look at Meatball!"

Meatball beamed at us as he drifted slowly past, and then the skateboard planted him headfirst into a giant flower bush on the other side of the driveway. His paws flailed as he backed himself out, shaking his butt vigorously.

Rebekah's parents came out of the garage, blinking in the sunlight. Her dad was wiping his hands on a rag, and her mom was brushing sawdust off her jeans.

"Watch Meatball," Rebekah said, pointing. "He can ride a skateboard! Eric, you didn't tell me he could do that! That's so cool!"

"I had no idea!" I said. "He's never seen one before, as far as I know."

Meatball finally disentangled himself from the bush and thoughtfully pawed at his face for a second. He looked around, spotted the skateboard, and pounced on it. But instead of riding it, he wrapped one paw over the top, lay down, and started chewing on the edge with his big floppy mouth.

"Meatball!" I said sternly, hurrying over to pull the skateboard away.

"That's OK, he can have it," Rebekah said. "Right, Mom?"

"Sure. We were just going to throw it out," her mom answered.

I squatted in the driveway next to Meatball. "You big dope," I said to him. "Do you want a skateboard? Is that what you're telling me?"

Yarm yarm yarm went his mouth against the side of the board. He rolled his eyes expressively toward me.

I touched the glittery lightning stickers. "Does it *have* to be pink?" I asked him.

Yarm yarm yarm.

"So this is your doggy Nintendo," I said thoughtfully. Teaching Meatball to ride the skateboard could be fun. It definitely wouldn't be boring! I pulled the skateboard out of his grasp and sent it rolling across the driveway. Meatball lunged to his feet and barreled after it, snorting. He pounced on it and it flew out from under his paws.

Rebekah laughed at his bewildered face. "Let's go to the park," she suggested. "You can pick up the skateboard on the way home."

"Thanks," I said, catching Meatball's leash.

He sat down and his tongue rolled out the side of his mouth. Uh-oh. I recognized that look.

Rebekah took Noodles and started down the driveway. I tried to follow her, but of course Meatball had decided not to budge. He didn't want to leave his new beloved pink soul mate behind.

I tugged sternly on my end of the leash. "Meatball, come!"

Snaarrr snaarrr snaarrrrr, went Meatball. His butt was rooted to the sidewalk.

I pulled harder, trying to drag him. Nothing doing.

Rebekah turned, halfway down the driveway, and saw that I was still stuck in place. I wanted to jump into one of the flower bushes myself. Why did I always look like such an idiot in front of her?

"Come on Meatball!" Rebekah called. He cast a longing glance at the skateboard. His message was clear: *Want it. Not moving until I have it.*

"I'm sorry," I said. "He always does this."

"Oh, it's OK, this is an easy problem," Rebekah said, coming back toward me. She reached into her bag and pulled out a handful of dog treats.

Meatball's ears perked up.

"You call him," she said, handing them to me. I waved a treat in Meatball's direction.

"Meatball, come," I said again.

He leaned toward me, sniffing, and then made a grab for the treat, but I pulled it away and stepped back. With a long-suffering sigh, Meatball got to his paws and followed me. After two steps I gave him the treat. At the end of the driveway, I gave him another.

He trotted agreeably next to me the rest of the way to the park, glancing up at my hand occasionally.

Note to self, I thought. *Take treats* everywhere *we go.*

"I should warn you," I said to Rebekah, "Meatball is kind of boring at the park."

She laughed. "With a face like that, Meatball could never be boring."

Meatball shot me a look like *Yeah, so there.*

I glanced at Rebekah and suddenly realized how totally crazy this was. If you'd told me just one week before that I'd be walking down the street with my own dog on one side of me and Rebekah Waters on the other, I wouldn't have believed you. I would never have imagined this could happen to me. Maybe to some other, braver, alternate-universe version of Eric.

OK, so I wasn't quite brave enough yet to ask Rebekah to be my girlfriend. But maybe with Meatball's help, one day I would be.

And sure, Meatball wasn't exactly the athletic dog of my dreams. There wasn't anything I could do about his snoring. Or his drooling. Or the fact that he sounded like a freight train when he breathed. But Meatball was loyal and funny and he helped me to be braver than I usually am. And you know what? It's not like I'm perfect either.

He looked up at me, snorting and rolling along on his fat paws, and grinned. It was like he could read my mind.

I guess you knew it all along, Meatball, I thought. *You are exactly the right dog for me.*

Yeti is a great dog . . . when he isn't getting into trouble!

Pet Trouble

Oh No, Newf!

T.T. SUTHERLAND

SCHOLASTIC

Turn the page for a sneak peek!

We could hear shouting from the sixth-grade hallway as we went through the front doors, and I could tell that one of the people shouting was Rory Mason. Rory is one of my best friends.

Then I realized that the other person shouting was Avery, and I was like, *Oh, no.* Every time Avery gets in trouble at school, his parents get supermad and then there's even *more* yelling and fighting, and then he's grumpy for months afterward. So you'd think he would try harder not to get in trouble, but sometimes it's like trouble just falls on him. I don't mean, like, accident trouble, like what happens to me. I mean, if someone's going to pick a fight or if someone's going to get blamed for something, it's probably Avery.

Also, I know Rory, and she pretty much says what she really thinks, and she would totally not be afraid of hitting him. Plus I didn't need my best friend and my secret friend hating each other's guts. It's hard enough to stop Avery from complaining about everyone at school.

"She says you took it, Avery!" Rory yelled as we came up to the crowd that was standing around our lockers. I saw Rory's little stepsister, Cameron, standing behind her, looking all mad, so I figured that was the "she" Rory was talking about. That meant real trouble because Rory is like a Rottweiler about defending Cameron.

"I didn't!" Avery yelled back. "She's lying!"

"Cameron wouldn't lie!" Rory shoved him in the chest.

"Yeah!" Cameron yelled. "So there! Meanie!"

"I don't need her stupid lunch money!" Avery shouted. He looked really upset. His green polo shirt was coming untucked and he kept clenching and unclenching his fists. I know that makes him look like he's about to punch someone, but I think it actually means he's trying to stop himself from getting too mad.

"Give it back, Avery!" Danny called.

I thought that was kind of unfair. We didn't even know the whole story yet.

I know, he's a bully and he says mean things and he likes making other people as miserable as he is.

But he's not a liar, and he's not a thief. I was pretty sure about that.

"Yeah Avery, stop being a jerk!" Tara Washington shouted. Like she should talk, by the way. She is *absolutely* as mean as Avery when she wants to be.

Then Brett Arbus poked his nose in and offered to buy Cameron's lunch in his smiley, slippery way.

"It's not about the money," Rory said. "It's about pushing around a little girl! What kind of freak-show coward are you, Avery?"

Well, OK. So then I had to get involved. Didn't I? I mean, poor Avery, if he was innocent. Or if he wasn't, then Rory needed my help.

I jumped in and grabbed Avery's arm. "Stop fighting!" I said. "You guys are both going to get in trouble again!"

"I didn't steal any stupid lunch money," Avery growled, glaring at Rory.

"Cameron says he did!" Rory insisted. "Why would she lie about that?"

I had to admit that was pretty confusing. "Maybe there's a mistake," I said. "Hey Cameron, did you maybe just lose it?"

"No!" Cameron said, pouting. Cameron is a very cute third-grader, with perfect pale skin and vibrant red curls. But I'm afraid being that cute helps her get away with anything. I mean, I would never tell Rory that her sister is a bit spoiled, but . . . she kind of is.

"It was in my backpack and then it was gone! He took it!" Cameron said decisively.

"Out of your backpack?" Rory said. "I thought you said he took it from you."

So it could be a mistake. I tried to give Avery a reassuring look, but he was too busy scowling at Cameron to meet my eyes.

"He did!" Cameron said. "It was mine!"

"But did you see him take it out of your backpack?" I asked.

Cameron's blue eyes were filling with tears, but I've seen her do that lots of times to get what she wants, so I wasn't sure it was all that real. "I know he did!" she cried. "I know he took it! He's mean!"

I couldn't really argue with that, but I could see that Rory was confused, too. She'll do anything for Cameron, but she's also really fair. I knew she wouldn't have accused Avery if she hadn't been sure he did it. And now she wasn't so sure.

That's when we heard the dreaded sound of Vice Principal Taney's voice.

"What is all this?" he barked, hurrying toward us. He looked *really* mad, almost as mad as when

someone hit him with a piece of bologna during the cafeteria food fight a couple weeks earlier. I felt like my feet were frozen in place. It was like someone just piled a whole pack of Great Danes on my shoulders. I was too terrified to move. I *hate* getting in trouble, because then Mom shakes her head and looks even more disappointed in me than usual.

Rory and Avery and Cameron were stuck there, too, but everyone else vanished.

Mr. Taney has long, bony fingers. He was waggling one of them at us like he was hoping it would turn us all into salamanders.

"Sir, it's just a misunderstanding," I said as fast as I could. "Really, there's nothing wrong, everyone's —"

"Detention!" Mr. Taney shouted. "All of you!" He stopped in front of us. His white hair was sticking up in grouchy tufts.

"All of us!" Cameron squeaked, looking outraged. "That's not fair! *I* didn't do anything! I'm a good girl!"

Mr. Taney pointed his bony forefinger at her little button nose. "Detention," he snarled. He pointed it at Rory, then Avery, then me. "Detention. Detention. Detention."

"Can't we explain?" Rory started to say, but Mr. Taney cut her off.

"My office. Lunch," he snapped. "And you all have after-school detention for the next week."

"A whole *week*!" Cameron shrieked.

"Push me, and I'll make it two," Mr. Taney hissed. "Now get to class."

So that's how I ended up in detention with Rory and Avery after school that Thursday. It wasn't really my fault, right? But maybe it's good that I was there, because Rory and Avery kept throwing each other these fierce hostile looks, and I'm not sure they could have stayed quiet that whole time if I wasn't sitting in between them trying to block the angry vibes.

And in some ways, it's definitely good that I got detention, because of what happened on the way home.

Avery rocketed out of his seat the minute Mr. Guare told us we could go. I don't even think he stopped at his locker. He shot out the front door of the school, practically leaving puffs of smoke behind him, like a cartoon.

Rory and Cameron walked me to my locker and then stood well back so nothing would fall out of it onto their heads. I don't have *any idea* how my locker becomes so messy so quickly, but I never have time to clean it, and anyway at least I know everything's in there somewhere. I hope.

"You want a ride home?" Rory asked me as I untangled my sweater from my math book and spilled jelly beans all over the hall. "I can't promise it'll be fun. Dad's not happy at all."

"It's not my *fault*," Cameron said for the eightieth time. "Avery's mean. I *know* he took my lunch money."

Rory didn't bother answering her.

"That's OK," I said. "I brought my bike today."

"All right," Rory said, pulling her ponytail tighter. "See you tomorrow, Heidi. Sorry about detention."

"It's no big deal," I said. "I finished most of my homework, so it's not all bad." I smiled at Rory to show her I knew it wasn't her fault.

Rory took Cameron's hand and they went off down the hall toward Coach Mason's office. I wrestled with my locker until I got it shut and then I went out the front door and unlocked my bike. It was the last one there. I hung my shiny blue helmet on the handlebars and pushed it across the street.

There's a big field across from the school with a track running around it, which grown-ups use a lot for exercise. You can usually find someone jogging there, wearing sweatpants and headphones and a determined look, but this afternoon it was empty. Trees and thick bushes grow around the edges, hiding the field from the streets around it, and there's a big space in the middle that the town uses for summer sports. I play soccer there a lot.

My bike went *bump bump bump* over the dirt as I pushed it toward the low wall that runs along one side of the track, under the trees. Avery was sitting on the wall, throwing stones at a tree trunk. Sometimes he waits for me there so we can walk home together.

"I have this great idea," he said as I walked up. "Let's take that lunch money I 'stole' and run away to New York and never come back."

"I know you didn't steal it," I said. I dropped my bike on the grass and hopped up on the wall next to him. "Are your parents going to be really mad?"

"Well, Dad's staying in a hotel again this week," Avery said, "so maybe she won't tell him, since they're 'not speaking.' But Mom. . . ." He threw another stone, really hard, and it bounced off the bark with a *clunk*.

"Maybe if you explain it to her . . . that it was a mistake . . ." I said. "I can talk to her if you want."

"Whatever," Avery said. "It's not worth it. If she wants to get mad, fine. I don't care. That stupid little *brat*." He jumped down, picked up a handful of rocks, and tossed them all at once. *Blip blip bonk bonk bonk* they went as they pinged off the tree and scattered to the ground.

"Why do you think Cameron said it was you?" I asked.

Instead of answering, he shoved his hand in his pocket, pulled out a small white object, and tossed it at me. I lunged to catch it and would have fallen off the wall, but Avery caught my arms and pushed me back up.

"There you go, throwing yourself at me again," he said, rolling his eyes.

"Thanks," I said with a grin, peering at the thing in my hand. It was an eraser, little and white and shaped like a tiny white dog — some kind of terrier, I guessed, with a red collar around its neck and a little pink tongue hanging out. "This is so cute," I said.

"I thought you'd like it," Avery said with a shrug. I looked up in surprise, and he went, "Don't get all mushy-wushy on me, Heidi. I found it on the playground yesterday. Problem is, the brat saw it at the same time and she pitched a fit when I wouldn't let her have it. Anyway, I guess that's why she's mad at me."

"Wow," I said, flipping the eraser between my fingers. "So you won this in a fight with an eight-year-old girl. No *wonder* I have such a crush on you."

"Shut up," he said, grabbing my foot and pulling off my sneaker.

"Give that back!" I yelled as he ran off across the field. "I'm not going to chase you with one shoe, Avery! Get back here!"

"What, this?" he called, stopping several feet away. He tossed my shoe from one hand to the other. "You want this?"

I crossed my arms. "I'm not going to come after it," I said.

"OK," he said with a shrug. "Then we can just stay here forever. Suits me. *I* don't want to go home."

Rrrrrrooorrrroorrrrrooooooo.

I tilted my head at Avery. "Did you just growl at me?" I asked. I was sure I'd heard something — something like a growl or a whimper or a mumble. Had it come from the bushes by the wall?

"You're losing it, Heidi," Avery said, wiggling his finger by the side of his head like I was crazy.

"You didn't hear that?"

"I didn't hear anything," he said with another shrug. He tossed my shoe behind his back and caught it in his other hand, then waved it at me.

"Avery, give me back my sneaker."

"Nope," he said, dancing back another step.

"You're a pain in my butt," I said.

"That's why you're in looooooooove with me," he said. "Hey, do you know you're wearing two different-colored socks?"

I looked down and realized that my shoeless foot was wearing a dark blue sock, while the other one was wearing a yellow sock with black polka dots. How did I do that? I must have been in such a hurry that morning that I didn't even notice.

"Yeah, I did that on purpose," I said.

"Sure you did," he said.

"If you don't give me back my shoe right now," I said, "I'm going to tell everyone at school that *you're* secretly in love with *me*."

"Like anyone would believe that, when I'm so far out of your league," Avery said, but he was frowning. "Hey, I have an idea. Since you like dogs so much, how about, if you want it — then you can fetch it!" He turned and threw my sneaker as hard as he could. It flew up in a huge arc, up and up and up and way out across the field.

"Avery!" I shouted, but then suddenly there was a huge rustling sound, and something exploded out of the bushes. A blur of black-and-white fur flew out, shot past Avery, and zoomed across the grass. Before my sneaker even hit the ground, the fur blur was half-way to where it was going to land.

I gasped.

It was a dog — the biggest, furriest dog I'd ever seen.

Avery's mouth was wide open. I'm sure mine was, too. We stared as the dog pounced on my sneaker, wrapped his massive jaws around it, and came trotting back toward us. His glorious black tail swung back and forth like a giant flag in a parade. He held his head up high and his long fur swished shaggily as he pranced over the grass.

He was *gorgeous.*

The dog trotted right past Avery and over to me. He was so huge, his head was even with my knees even though I was sitting up on a wall. The dog dropped my sneaker right in my lap, nudged my knee with his nose, and looked up at me with the biggest, softest brown eyes I'd ever seen. A long pink tongue hung out of his mouth and he looked like he was smiling all over his shaggy black face.

My heart nearly leaped out of my chest when he looked at me. It was like we could read each other's minds, and they were saying the same thing: *Hey there, best friend.*

How can one Pet cause so much Trouble?

Runaway Retriever

Loudest Beagle on the Block

Mud-Puddle Poodle

Bulldog Won't Budge

Read the series and find out!

For more great dog stories, be sure to check out

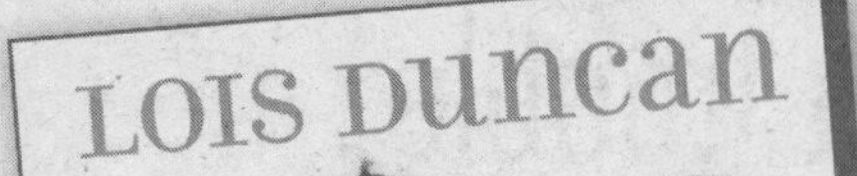

AND DON'T MISS THE EXCITING SEQUEL . . .